CW01260908

**WRECKING BALL PRESS
HULL • ISSUE 4**

the reater

EDITOR & WHIP CRACKER

SHANE RHODES

Design & Cover Illustration   by   Owen Benwell

With special thanks to: Jules Smith • Claire Hutchings •
• The very reverend Newdick • Russell Jones •
Keith Angel • Graham Hamilton

©All Copyright remains with the artists & contributors.
Unless for the purposes of review or drunken recitation do not attempt to reproduce any part of this periodical.

This edition of the reater has been funded by

All submissions, subscriptions,
and any other material should be sent to :
The Reater
9 Westgate
North Cave
Brough
East Yorkshire
HU15 2NG

Published in 2000 by Wrecking Ball Press

table of contents

gerald locklin
- jackson pollock: one: number 31, 1950..................15
- the motive..................16
- starting point..................17
- hilary and jackie..................18
- the boulevard de clichy..................19
- montmatre..................20
- the ile grande jatte..................22
- his sanity..................23

martin mooney
- ice..................27
- a day procedure..................28

julian turner
- legends..................35
- some mate for life..................36
- the magnificent history of the english..................38

steve dearden
- prarie hoisters - calgary..................43
- rocky mountains - banff..................45

k. m. dersley
- rutter's chance..................49
- selling himself good..................50
- the gospel according to him..................51

peter lewin
- liam..................55
- who knows when?..................56
- pepi!..................57

linda rocheleau
- shopping in toronto..................61
- farmhouse at bath..................62

(painting by **jayne jones**)

lawrence bradby
    an autumn visit..69
    speculation..70

geoff hattersley
    chicken bone charlie...75
    splinter..76
    ongoing..77
    race relations on the shop floor....................................78
    lee's dog..79
    i did brain surgery on a barnsley pub floor.................80
    poem for tony...81

anna robinson
    bubble moon...85
    first offence...86
    the storm..87

ken steedman
    in an empty house..91
    bridge.. 92

daithidh maceochaidh
    schrödinger's cat..97
    black kettle..98
    the man who mistook his wife for a twat.....................100

stephen wade
    the president's man...105

carol coiffait
    reginald dixon is alive and well in lincolnshire............121
    drosophila - feral male/female......................................122

(painting by **jayne jones**)

ben myers
    box-star bobby..129
    the turnbuckle larceny..132
    you are the gallery..137

joan jobe smith
- shane, coming back..147
- have i told you lately that i love you........................148
- when gentlemen preferred go-go girls.....................149
- lucky i wasn't wild wendy or dingy dina...................151
- woodchuck...153
- the star of david...154
- by the light of the silvery moon..............................156
- maureen o'hara...157

roddy lumsden
- lumsden hotel..161
- my water..162
- reconstruction...163
- my first crush..164

fred voss
- the voice of the woman who needs you....................169
- learning to love earplugs...170
- nuts and bolts and men..172
- one button off a dead son's shirt.............................173
- too big for tin walls to hold.....................................174
- cadillacs..175
- clearing the air..176
- he won't be on news at 5...177
- just what they wanted to hear.................................178
- going to his corner..179

peter didsbury
- peter didsbury interviewed by jules smith...............183
- mediaeval, somehow..197
- to warm a house..198
- therefore choose life..200
- the house sitter's letter...201

(painting by **jayne jones**)

s. waling
- we start with the sea..207

j. morris
    lines written more in anger than in sorrow......................208

edward michael o'durr supranowicz
    cops..210

alan catlin
    her t-shirt said..211

jonathan brookes
    blessed...212

s harvey
    gambling..214

jon summers
    los angeles or southampton.......................................216

keith valentine
    swarfega...217

geoff stevens
    epidemic...219

t.f. griffin
    frank...220

brad evans
    on the last night in spain...221

graham hamilton
    beneath black ven fossil cliffs - 1999
    (or one minute to midnight).......................................223

jonathan asser
    trick..227
    professional advice..228
    progression..229

edward field
    mirror songs..233

    in the mirror..234
    over fifty..236

brendan cleary
    the reunion..243
    the neighbour..244
    the debate...245
    the economy..246

joseph allen
    mcfaul's day..251
    the foreman...252

(painting by **jayne jones**)

fiona curran
    jazz singer..259
    from the front...260

don winter
    cleaning up at the hamtrack burger chef.......................265
    saturday night desperate..266

michael gregg michaud
    tim's wife becomes a lesbian and a yoga instructor.........271
    in defense of voyeurism..273

peter knaggs
    in praise of tin openers..277
    the door bell is ringing...279
    a man on chanterlands avenue slices an onion................280
    sam thumbs a spent cartridge twenty years after...........281

dean wilson
    the king and i..285
    shopping 1..286
    shopping 2..287
    shopping 3..288

giovanni malito
    cityscape #12..293

don't cry for me, suburbia..294
atlas should shrug..296

susan maurer
lemurs..301
starstreak..302
mackie hill, miami, arizona...303

reviews.....305

gerald locklin
Long Beach, USA

jackson pollock: one: number 31, 1950

suddenly we realize that this is everything:
the universe, the self, the molecules,
their nuclei, motion, rest, the stars,
desire, shakespeare, color, absence, heat
and light, anxiety, the umbilical telephone,
the beast and beauty, chaos, order,
stimulus, perception, the creative,
virginia woolf, the waves, emotion,
monasteries, christ and shiva,
music, wagner, bach, miles, coltrane,
philip glass and seymour, dna,
the life of the senses,
the life of the mind,
life, literature, lifelessness,
death, time, eternity,
the teapot in the tempest,
control and spontaneity,
space, boundlessness, boundaries,
you name it.

it's all here.
all language.
all there is to see.
all there is to hear.
all there is to think.

sleep never stops.

the motive

as a writer you get to seek
popularity or immortality,
riches or fame,
rewards for your labor
in this life or the next.

it's highly unlikely
you'll achieve both.
the nature of originality
tends to render the two
mutually exclusive.

of course the strongest odds
are that you'll end up
with neither.

i've got to go, though,
with the idea that
the life force is always
the driving force within
the greatest artists
because the life force is,
after all,
what the greatest art
is always all about.

starting point

it occurs to me
while walking with my wife and dog
along a dusty mountain road
why we worry about things
(don't you? i do.)
that we'll never live to see,
like the sun burning down
or the ocean drying up –

it's the selfish gene in us
that cares,
the one that wants to live
forever.

i tell my wife this,
and she says, "we care about
the world our kids and grandkids
and their kids will live in,
because we love them so."

and i agree,
but i suspect
that it's the selfish gene
that makes it possible
for us to love unselfishly.

hilary and jackie

of course i loved the film:

i have had ample lifetime
to observe both sibling rivalry
and sibling loyalty,
competition and differentiation,
the force of birth order,
the shock and lifelong sadness
of dethronement.

i have known the love of sisters,
for each other
and by me.

i have known the love of london
and the love of wales.

i have loved concerti
of the cello,
elgar, dvorak,
and the women
who play them.

of course i loved the film.

the boulevard de clichy

what is the difference
between his boulevard
and those of caillebotte?

his is not grand, nor is
the focus on the fashionable.

his is less populated, and the
people aren't out for a stroll –
they're hurrying to get someplace.

his is a thoroughfare of
molecules in motion, of which the
pedestrians are only a part.

he sees like the scientist,
not like the journalist.

mondrian will abstract,
in different cities,
from his verticality of structures,
his horizontal arteries.

the earth is encircled by winds,
even the urban concentrations,
warmed and cooled by them,
and counter to their turning.

the paris night belongs to
hemingway, toulouse-lautrec, my memories:
he painted mornings.

montmartre

i wish i'd been alive
when it was still a butte
of vegetable gardens, ramshackle
sheds, and functioning windmills
above the moulin rouge, when
agriculture was still a part of
the urban, when the peasant
lived not far from the factory
worker, or was the same person.

but i'm a creature of nostalgia,
regretful that i arrived in southern
california after the days of
film noir, the real hollywood,
although there was still a lot of
wasteland between l.a. and long
beach in 1964, and dairy valley
wasn't yet cerritos, and citrus
groves still lined the boulevards
of orange county, and the strawberry
fields had not given way to the
corporate headquarters of mitsubishi,
hyundai and toyota.

and could the light of
paris really be that bluer,
airier, than in the lowlands?
or are we talking atmosphere,
the expanding horizon of the
artist, the seeming escape
from the provinces, the
parochial, the impoverishment, to
the gaiety of the capital
of the art world, the
cabarets, the centuries of
inspiration and accomplishment.

light or lightheadedness or a
light heart and a lightened burden,
all, no doubt, all: and the
unbearable lightness of being
young.

the île grande jatte

how have i managed to miss it?
probably i passed beneath the
bridge glassed in a *bateau mouche*
with my dozing children,
didn't catch the announcement
in french from the crackling speaker.
maybe they didn't bother to announce
it out of the tourist season,

seurat, van gogh, sondheim,
for starters. i guess today it's
condos anyway, and the
seine a lot like the l.a. river,
channeled in concrete for flood control,
not life-sustaining water bordered
by banks of vegetation, ducks and geese,
the leaves of autumn changing colors
on the ordinary trees. the
insignificance of the individual
is no longer even a theme,
just taken for granted now.

his sanity

of the seventy paintings
in this exhibition, perhaps
five are famous. it's the
others that strike one most,
in their simple painterly skill,
their originality of subject and treatment,
most of all in their *lack*
of "madness."

the thinness, for instance, of the
brushstrokes delineating a flowerpot
of chives. i don't remember
ever viewing a pot of chives
before. i joke to my wife that
he must have created them to
sprinkle on the ubiquitous
potatoes: baked? you know
that dairy cows will turn
up (turnip?) to provide
the sour cream.

trust me: this is a very
well painted pot of chives,
a million dollar pot of
chives, a pot of chives
you wouldn't be bored with
on your wall, a pot of
chives more endearing, in
certain ordinary ways, then, say,
a pot of electric irises,

an eminently *sane* pot of chives,
and yet far more than
merely competently rendered.

martin mooney
Belfast, Northern Ireland

Ice

i.m. Paddy McArdle

When morphine constipates him
a neighbour tells him ice will free his bowels.
His wife feeds ice-cubes one by one
inside him till at last he squeezes out
a tiny, blood-dark frozen stool-

ice, mostly, though his belly feels
as though it's hard-pressed snow, a rock
of pack-ice frozen to his spine.
Another patient at the hospice tells him-

'If it wasn't for the call of nature, some
of us would never walk again.'

A Day Procedure

Reasons

To think, after two difficult births, a job,
late nights, alcohol, and growing older-
    in no particular order-

that what had lain behind our torpid sex-life
wasn't physical distaste, or boredom
    but a dislike of condoms-

and you, who I'd thought cold, or disinterested
reminded me without speaking of the risk
    you'd run with the pill,

the embolism, the circulatory damage
that still caused trouble even now, and convinced me
    to set a vasectomy

against the so-far-to-me-imaginary pleasure
of ejaculation felt inside one's own body,
    the warm spill you said

was the most intimate of the intimate
pleasures we had been neglecting, the secret
    worth a cut, a stitch.

Net

In the end, we didn't download
the pictures filed on some doctor's website
of vasectomies gone skew-whiff,

so that I never winced at what
they'd call a post-op complication,
that blackened, bled-into scrotum,

a ballbag big as a goat's. Thank God
we settled, for a rake, on shots
of women giving pigs and horses head.

Prep

I always left my homework to the last minute.
On the morning of the op, I bathe
as per instructions, gingerly pluck
a fold of scrotum-skin and stretch it taut.
If you'd seen the mess I make of my chin
the odd morning I bother to shave,
you'd understand my reluctance
to take the razor to the recommended inch-
square patch of pube on either side.
Furl and wrinkle, fold and pleat-
enough gooseflesh to hide my face in.

Op

The sense of touch versus the sense of sight.
I stare at the lamp
while he rifles my purse
and pray to be kept in the dark,

the surgeon's rummage
like the frisk
of bran-tub or lucky-bag
by a blindfold child.

'Yon antrin thing'

The road from the hospital is also the road from the airport.
The road from anywhere is also the road 'to'.
I drove this one night in fog so thick
my headlights spent themselves six inches from the car.
My friend drives me home after the procedure.
The hills are in their post-thunderstorm
varnish, behind the hills a rainbow that isn't-
a long horizontal smear, an aurora, a broad brushstroke
the like of which we've never seen before.

Paisley too

This is Paisley country, its cattle marts and church halls
cringing beneath and calling down the thunder.
Big Ian's also in the hospital,
the Tele says: a urinary (not a gospel) tract
infection, as if from years of taking the piss....
the Party says he'll be back in action soon,
firing quote unquote on all cylinders.

Arnica

Two pillules of arnica
dissolve under my tongue,
metallic and as sweet
as birthday cake sugar-balls,

which suggest in turn
skateboard ball-bearings loosed
from their fixed orbit, pearls
from a snipped necklace.

'For the relief of bruising
and inflammation.'
My right testicle looks
like an eyeball hidden

behind an old woman's
heavily made-up lid,
its blended blue-black, red
and purple no disguise.

Something's been hurt.
I want to lie more akimbo
than my hips allow.
I am bruised and permanently

horny, half-erect, stung
by the post-operative throb
into desire. Darwin, take arnica,
the horse has bolted.

One week later

The sutures dissolve-
just this cat's whisker
pricked among the stubble
on my right plum.

Who knows what signals
it's picking up now:
the shortsleeved women
of the new summer,

the radiant danger
of my two children
about to leap, all knees and
elbows, into my lap.

julian turner
Otley, England

Legends

I used to pray for Marc Bolan each Sunday
my head pressed to the tiny Phillips tranny
locked in my bedroom with *The Warlock of Love*
trying to trip on nutmeg and orange juice.
He made me feel so...mauve.

We got to dance on stage with him and Steve Took
at Fairfield Halls, Croydon; some in smocks
and kaftans, me in blue, high-waisted flares
and a mustard nylon poloneck from Fosters:
polyester of Glam Rock.

We'd amp-up in Twig's garage for 12-bar blues.
Forever missing the beat but making noise,
we all bragged about "bringing an album out",
clicking away with our Instamatics, always
writing the sleeve notes.

We were already on a loop orbit out
to the tortuously Weird - which translates as "fate"
I found out from my dad's *Germanic Myths*.
It seemed to fit though God knew what it meant.
We had nothing to steer with.

Some Mate For Life

Thanks for your letter. Is it really ten
years since we met? It seems like yesterday –
you on Port Meadow in your daffodil dress
with its distinctive markings, me the drab one;
our passion in the fug of evergreens
then luncheon in The Trout. I have to say
silk stockings still remind me of your knees.

All courtships follow their own protocol.
Ours did - we both knew putting one foot wrong
is lethal. We observed the proscribed zones,
the prescribed rituals: visual display, touch,
vibration and the surge of pheromones.
I did my best although I'm only male.
It was all over by the end of lunch.

It's true, the world misunderstands our sort.
They haven't got a clue about such things.
In fact it's rare for fit males to be caught
by lines of silk, although your *Argiope*
may start eating him while they are mating.
I'm grateful this has not occurred to me.
I watch the eyes of lovers for that look.

It's all so dreamy - I recall your palps.
languorous and svelte, could I forget
the way you held yourself rigid, your small gulps,
how the burrs adhered to your long legs,
your light hairs standing to the touch of wind,
the way you seemed to *thrum*? I picture it,
a silver hook which won't let go my mind.

I had to move from Oxford years ago.
There are no soul-mates here. I hope I can
confess to you, who I still feel I know,

the bald verbs of my mid-life: fuck and eat -
and in between a narrowing horizon,
a sharper focus where these two words meet
like friends who have been parted for too long.

The Magnificent History of the English

My aunt has cooked me four lamb chops for tea.
She waves the mint sauce. Like a magician
she stands in strip-light clenching and unclenching
her freckled, arthritic hands on empty air.

Together, we have trawled through the photo albums
and found Ida - the great aunt I remember
shrunk beside the fire-place in Hitchin, half-hidden
by the tall-boy, her hands afraid like birds.

But in these tiny snaps she's young again,
even happy-looking. Here she is with Bud –
her pet name for my aunt - her rusty, damaged
blade of a face suddenly lit from within.

She was how my aunt survived the cold
touch of her own mother who only saw her son,
who lavished love on him, the boast of Arlesey
at her bridge parties, and who gave her none.

Towards the end of Ida's album Tom
appears, his bland disguise of tennis whites
conceals his marriedness, the way he had
her in the potting shed, the fists of his knees,

and other men: the Revd. Knightly in
the bucket seat of "the good old Morris Cowley",
tennis with doctors from the loony bin,
and Cecil Soundry shaving in his vest.

On the inside back cover Bud stands
squinting up at the sun. She holds a wand
of bracken. With her other arm she looks
for Ida who bends down to fill her hand.

My aunt carries out the bones. She locks
the door on distant memory with relief.
We both look down the long corridor, and laugh
at the fucked Turners, English as roast beef.

steve dearden
Leeds, England

Prarie Hoisters - Calgary

I step for my Haircut Anytime! into a brown any place maybe the first person in forty years. The barber, no taller standing up from his own chair points, "You read a lot of pork?"

I say, "Pork?"

"Yeh," he say, "You read pork." Steers me onto the cracked leather, grey capes me, tucks knuckles under my collar.

We establish English, Lebanese, agree a skin cut, my bristle joining the grey filings clogged in his clippers, I scuff where he missed a buzz above my ear. On the formica counter a black and white box TV, Musharraf deposes Sharif, a peace keeper lies dead in leafy Kosovo.

"They should never go in." He say, "They don't know the roos."

"Roos?"

"Roos."

I ask, "You been back to Beirut?"

"No, too damn heart." Fans himself. "And for you in England, eh? All these grills."

"Grills?"

"Yeh, grills." He slaps a folded Globe and Mail across my knees, "Teenage pregnancies are concentrated in the North of England where joblessness, poverty and hopelessness are endemic."

He shrugs sympathy, shakes my dust from the cape, hands me my Chapters bag, "Enjoy your porks."

I pick up a Red Top, the driver over here three years from Pakistan, we trade Lahore driving stories: the rickshaw sandwich - one slice ox-cart, the other 4x4. Back at the Crow Trail Best Village Hotel, I search for a rupee tip, come up with dollars and sense.

Rocky Mountains - Banff

Banff could be Ilkley with bigger rocks if it weren't for the old dears like Elke, on the town with her sisters, high haunching, loping their fur-ringed bums down Main Street, asking for it, stopping the traffic, Hot for trot. Born for horn. Strutting for a rutting.

And Ilkley could be Banff were its springs sulphur, its pools lounge pools, steaming pools, lie back watching the sun set over ice peaks pools, rather than o o o ice cold lunge out as fast as you plunge in pools.

Could be. If our rails ran right through and beyond the valley, freight slower than walking, longer than a stroll. Freight calling - not a whistle not a hooter not a klaxon nor Elke, deep in the woods - but a coming "you're welcome", passing "no rush", right through "back soon" blat. Far off inside us.

k. m. dersley
Ipswich, England

Rutter's Chance

Toby Rutter had a book out
from a reputable Northern firm.
Not one of these fly-by-nights,
the concern was known for heavy writing
and a firm foundation of art.
All these verse epistles he spun out, informing one
Eunice
of how he'd like to fly
by the seat of *her* pants.

He put it well in those poems
some of them 17 years avintage
and. they still read fresh
because red hot writing stays toasty.
Middle aged, he can still give it a go.
His girlfriend says he sounds like Barry White

to me he more resembles one of the old
actor-managers.

All his writing about Clacton and wherever
and he has this knack of making Ipswich
(another of his ports of call) a place
where nobody would ever tend to die.

It's not too much to say his outpourings
could well bring Joyce to mind –
yes, Joyce who used to work in
Harry Nugent's grocery right up
unto our own mothers' day
though the place is now a Charity Shop.

This writing of Rutter's I take
to be the real stuff like Chaucer's stint –
the race's memory.
Even what they refer to
as the authentic gossiping on paper.

Selling Himself Good

ryk riches is an artist and all
over the world he's gone
wailing
gabbling
and waltzing about the stage-
the Dutch like it particularly,
and the Scandinavians. (It surmounts the
language barrier, like
Chaplin of old.)

We had a bloke here from Belgium who
organised a display of rocks and
stones outside the Mansion for a few
thousand smackers.
I saw him staring at his handiwork with
a finger to his lips, then
moving this stone or that
to one side or the other. He
didn't have a
clue what he was doing.

ryk gets his thousands too,
all sorts of grants and Bursaries
and he runs courses and Workshops
that bring in a lot more
than you get cold-selling
or thrashing a word
processor at County Hall.

There he is on stage, not much hair,
pony tail, 'partner' not bad-looking,
and I think yes, he's really
in touch with something.
He must network skilfully all right,
and one of those helping
must be the Prince
of This World.

The Gospel According To Him

Eventually we have to live up to our failings
and sometimes when Cliff couldn't take any more
he'd go out and spend money on one of the prostitutes
he used to give a lift to
he'd get one back to the Boat Yard where he lives in
his Mini and she'd start by getting her top off
and that was just because of all the lifts he'd given her
and her friends and he'd pay some money for the etcetera
and get glassy-eyed with the urge rolling about with her
before calling her cunt and telling her in spirit
he could see a lump of greasy meat on her left breast
and who was that white-haired woman standing by her shaking
her head, was it Gran?
He knows it's not pretty but he's a man of some sensibility
and he often won't entertain a soul, not even us:
'Stay away – your vibes are too strong, they'll kill me!'
he shrieks, wiping away the white ulcer jalap
rolling around in the wrappers that litter the
car with the back seat taken out
and the contraceptives filled with cotton wool
that he puts up his behind so the spirits can't get in
while he sleeps with another one over his 'penis hole'.

We all have to live up to our shortfalls
and Cliff Rawlings has fewer than some.

peter lewin
Preston, England

Liam

Thought he was Bukowski
Lenny Bruce and Jerry Lewis
all rolled into one:
in fact a real cool dude.
A pony tailed Poet in residence
shaggin all the little girls
(who knew no fucking better
but soon would) reading them
his poems in bed, saying
they were really deep.
"There's too many dickheads
writing these days he sez?

Who Knows When?

Another wet grey day and the man
who looked as fit as a fiddle
as dropped dead on the pavement.
He was a vegetarian, a jogger
a non smoker, a non drinker
and went to Church every Sunday.
His Missis cleans, hoovers every day.
It's like a show house, the wife says.
Anyway the Ambulance has carried him off
and loads of folk are gawping.
And I'm going to tuck into chips
gravy and jumbo sausages.
"Switch that fucking hoover off Luv
and get your mouth round this."

Pepi!

In broken English he says-
Hello! Hello! my name is Pepi!
I am going to show you round the Island.
Hello! Hello! attentioni!

Everybody come closer please!
Hello! Hello! attentioni!
Hello! Hello! my name is Pepi!
Pepi! Pepi!... we all reply.

Hello! Hello! attentioni!
when you see this umbrella
you will know where Pepi is.
Pepi! Pepi! we all shout.

He shoots off into the crowds-
his yellow umbrella twirling above heads.
Everyone shouting Pepi! Pepi!
and Hello! Hello!, trying to keep up.

linda rocheleau
Savannah, USA

Shopping in Toronto

The Portuguese woman returns silently
from market, hands buried beneath black crepe,
with a few pears for supper, a basket of sour wine,
some salted fish. The city shifts and usurps
the quiet boundaries of her neighborhood,
ornate iron fences painted black and white,
flower beds to brighten the sloping lawns.
BMW's dart in and out, their owners running
into boutiques with names like Nanny's Nook
or Hollycock's to snatch up the last of the silver
samovars brought over by aunts who once held
them between knees for the long crossing.
They polished engraved trumpet vines and muscatel
with the hems of their skirts. The woman's head
is slanted down, coarse skin ripened like the inside
of an oak cask curing black olives, the color
of draping to hide hair and shoulders once touched
by a man she will mourn for the rest of her life.
Beneath her heavy steps, the subway soars into
Eaton Center where ladies spread smoked salmon
and cream cheese on points of toast. After cappuccino
and current tarts, they will shop for cashmere and silk.
The widowed woman pours milk into a pitcher for her
thick evening tea, stares at its swirling leaves, taps a melody
on the speckled blue rims of her saucer and cup.

Farmhouse at Bath

You taught us to tease furtive
doodlebugs from their holes
with sticks of fresh cut indian brush.
We never caught one, but swept
their dreamless shadows from morning
to dusk beneath a canopy of oaks planted
by your five brothers at Bath. We pushed
a rusty one-hinged gate against the rank
smokehouse, curing only a nest of baby blue
wrens, their featherless bodies a hex on our
imaginations. My sister sat in awe. I carved
filmy eyes from a rooster's head. We built plank
temples adorned with dandelions in half-pints
and eggs stolen from angry hens. We served
milky concoctions to platinum-haired aunts
who shared their tales of the city: martini baths,
cigarettes smoked from mother-of-pearl wands.
You smiled. We shucked half bushels of corn,
city kid's fingers swelling from the stiff stalks.
The old farmhouse stands sagging and empty
beneath shade of overgrown pecan trees. The
cistern has gone dry, ground turned sour to clay.
Only a pale narcissus, planted by your mother fifty
years before, waves in the tall sweetgrass.

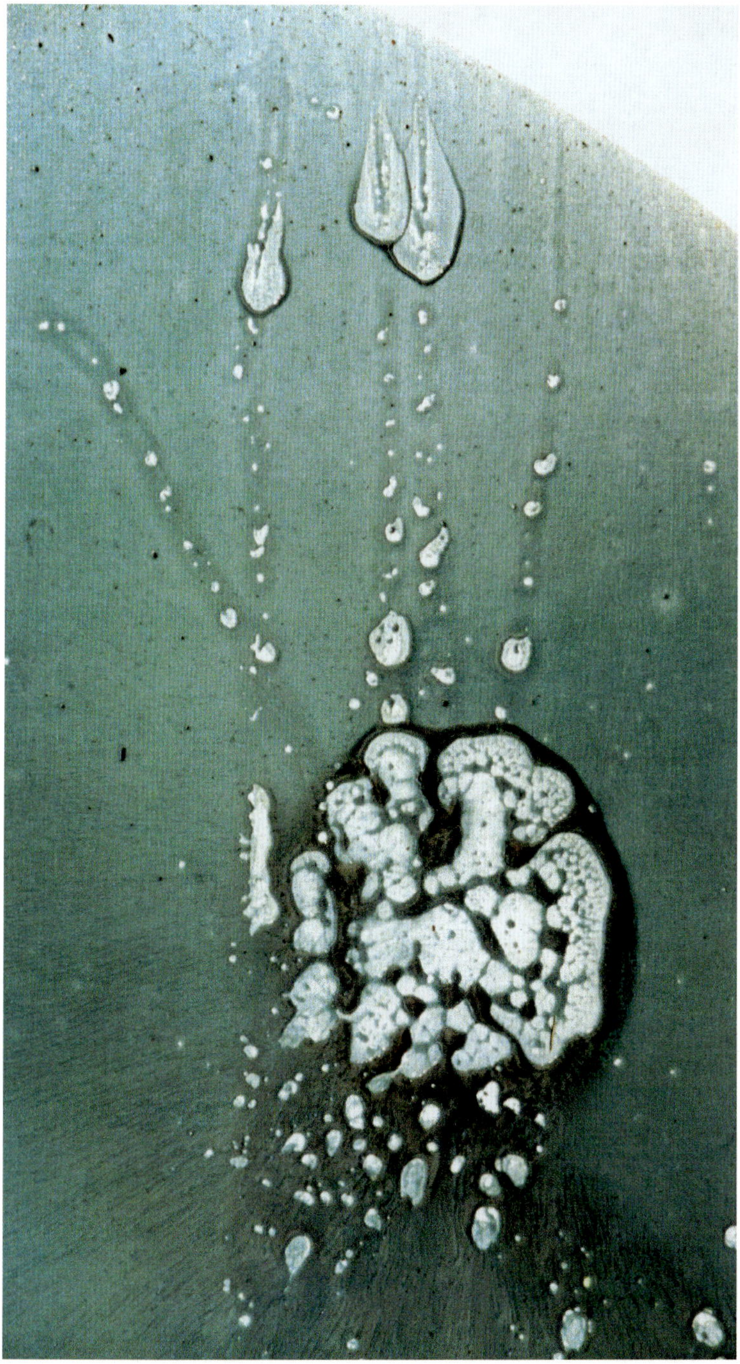

lawrence bradby
Norwich, England

An Autumn Visit

Lifting the latch I find the back garden just as empty.
I take the steep path to the shed and shelter there.

Clouds graze the pudding hills behind me, then press on;
Their rain is due inland.

Tartan and corduroy, the billowing fabric of fields
Is roped in by the creaking hedgerows.

Red marl slips its blanket another sticky inch
Down the shoulders of hills hunched over their secret insides

Skirting the high ground, the road seeks out the flat
Like an iron soothing folds.

Bursting like litter over the gardens, the flock of starlings
Is raked, fluttering, back to its roost by the wind.

I've waited long enough.
If she reads the signs she'll know I've called.

Speculation

As usual I've laid my newspaper aside,
Lost interest in the way Time shakes, shuffles
And refolds our lives; the paper world of politics.

I'm distracted by the railside clutter,
The endless indecipherables of gear
Assembled pending unknown jobs:
Forgotten coils of wire,
Oily wooden sleepers
Stacked in rough dolmens.
In slack rhythm, chanting the name of each item,
The train makes a soothing patter.

Container trucks catch my eye:
Sidelined in clots and strings
their logos hint at traveller's fabulations –
SeaLand, TransAnglian, Genstar -
Or incite some explanation -
Maersk, Uyundai, Cho Yang.
Patient cells intending to unpack and replicate themselves,
They'll manufacture reasons to be here, take over space,
Expand, (maybe starting from the vast rotting trackside sheds
Absurdly well-protected, razor-wire, portraits of snarling dogs)
Until the deckle-edge of each field is pinned down
By a shining factory unit, the gentle tucks
And smocking of the hills is gleaming,
Weeping like a bride in her longed-for gown.

A tunnel folds all that away,
replacing Ipswich goods yards
with the image of our carriage
reflected on dark glass.

Coming out of a cutting the train slows,
Eases to a stop, rocks back on its heels,

Whistles through its teeth. The lights flicker
Hum happily, the train is alert to signals unseen
Looking straight down the line and away from the sidings
Where more trucks are jammed like bold-type library books.
Their flanks are foxed with rust.

Those frantic twins, Finance and Industry
Shook these trucks here like spots from an ink pen that's blocked.
The pen's traced away from this page, is now writing
In margins of stories elsewhere.
The trucks have read, swallowed and forgotten
their secret instructions. And anyway

they are sliding from sight
as the trains pulls on.

Spreading my newspaper
a fresh sheet of my son's play-group artwork slips out,
his name clearly written at the top.
There's a busy central knot of colour
and stray lines wandering to the paper's edge.
I picture his waning interest as the lines start to intersect,
his grab at a clean sheet, and smile.

geoff hattersley
Huddersfield, England

Chicken Bone Charlie

The three lads in the bus station
are just about legless, shouting 'Barmy Army'
over and over
as we wait for the
Marsden Hard End. It's 7.28
on a Saturday evening. I'm on my way home
from work, a hard job made harder today
by the close company of Chicken Bone Charlie,
a scruffy-arsed little ragamuffin
who got on the wrong side of me
first thing in the morning
by playing a 90-minute Meat Loaf cassette
at full volume on his ghetto blaster.
We didn't speak from 7.15 a.m. to 6 p.m.,
despite working side by side. Then I said,
'Only one hour to go,' and he replied,
'Good. I'm sick of having to look at you.'
So I said, 'Even your best friend
must be sick of looking at you',
then neither of us
spoke again, as the last hour
dragged its clod-like feet.

Splinter
i.m.Mona Eileen Hattersley, 1935-1998

She said it was too small for her to see
and too small for my dad to see
but she had a splinter in her finger,

it was driving her up the wall –
this was when she was about fifty-five
so I was about thirty-four.

She passed me a pair of tweezers,
told me to take the splinter out
if I could see it. I could see it alright

and I got it with the tweezers
and pulled it straight out, no messing,
and my mother gave a sigh of relief.

Eight years later she was drugged up,
surrounded by flowers and cards,
fussed over by strangers in uniforms.

We took her home for the last month, she insisted.
'They can't make a proper cup of tea here,' she said,
'it's no wonder everybody's badly.'

Ongoing

It's strange to stand here
doing the most mundane job invented.
I've become a dab hand
with a very sharp knife.
There's time to fold my arms
and reflect as I wait for the machine
to complete its cycle
on how dull it is to do this.

We're treated like schoolboys.
There's a list of things we can't do.
No smoking. No eating.
No reading. No crosswords.
No lounging on the tables
as it presents a slovenly image
and damages the tables too.
We need permission to go for a piss.

It's strange to stand here
while share prices vacillate
and while marine biologists
eat sandwiches on warm beaches
and while cats stalk sparrows
in overgrown gardens
and while movie stars make movies
that are nothing like life.

Race Relations on the Shop Floor

We had a young Asian man start,
he only worked three or four days.

He sliced his thumb pretty badly
trimming lawnmower underdecks.

There was a lot of blood,
all over the table and floor.

I stood looking at it with Lee.
It was our job to clean it up.

Lee said he was surprised there was so much –
"Pakis don't like to part with owt, do they?"

For a while we had two Asian workers
known to most as "The Quiet Paki"

and "The Gobby Paki"
but they didn't last long either.

Lee's Dog

Lee brought his dog to work
because his dad had gone away
and the dog didn't like
being alone all day.
Christ, I said, it's a dog,
it doesn't have to like it,
what's it going to do,
pack a suitcase and leave?
Lee tethered it
outside the back door, right next
to where he was working
on the reject mouldings
granulating machine.
It was a huge, stupid-looking beast,
just the sort of dog
a halfwit like Lee would go for,
and it lay on its belly
in the sun all day
with its ugly tongue
lolling from its mouth.
Every time I ducked out
for a cigarette
the dog would be there.
I didn't come even close
to liking it
or anything like that.

I Did Brain Surgery On A Barnsley Pub Floor

Wayne by the juke-box lost an eye at the weekend,
Wayne watching Wayne and Wayne playing pool broke
both arms – he was complaining he couldn't wipe his
backside.

Wayne walked in with a dog's skull in the palm of his
hand – "Alas, poor Wayne, my fair sister," he said.
He sat down at the bar, in between Wayne and Wayne.

Wayne proposed a toast to Wayne, but Wayne, Wayne
and Wayne refused to drink and left in a bit of a huff.
"John Wayne films! I bloody well can't stand them!"

shouted Wayne, the uninjured one with the moustache.
I took my scalpel out and introduced myself -"Hello, I'm
a surgeon of some renown, Dr. Wayne..."

Poem For Tony

My drinking water is unfit for human consumption
and I can't stand Tony.
Thirty years ago they landed on the moon
and I can't stand Tony.
I'm tired of answering the phone
to people trying to sell me windows
and I can't stand Tony.
I've run out of cannabis and mushrooms
and I can't stand Tony.
Neighbourhood brats throw bricks at our front door
and I can't stand Tony.
I'm trying hard not to think about Tony
and I can't stand Tony
and I throw darts at pictures of Tony.
I'm working forty-eight hours in four days
and I can't stand Tony.
My wife prefers tea, I'd rather have coffee
and neither of us can stand Tony.
The bellringers across the road won't stop
and I haven't cleaned the fish tank
and I can't stand Tony.
There's never anything on the telly
and I can't stand Tony.
Tony can't stand people like me
and I can't stand Tony.
I don't have a hankie, my nose is blocked
and I can't stand Tony.
I can't play the ukelele
and I've never had any desire to
and I can't stand Tony
and I can't stand the ukelele
because Tony likes it.
And I can't stand Tony.

anna robinson
London, England

Bubble Moon

The night my mum kidnapped the local council
locking them in the back room of the Seven Feathers
Community Centre, we stayed at home,
me and my little sister Abigail
with our babysitter Ann-Marie, only
we weren't babies and that night was a full moon.

Ann-Marie said we shouldn't look
at it, so we did, then she said
especially not through glass, so my sister
ran into the kitchen and got every glass
in the cupboard and those in the washing-up bowl and brought
them all through. We looked at the moon through all of them;

tumblers, wine-glasses, a thick-bottomed tot glass, a brandy
bowl etched with the name Loretta, we added cracks
and chips to the craters and rilles, we projected
I Love Queen's Park Rangers from pyrex
across the Sea of Tranquility, we split the moon
into eight perfect little baby moons

with the bubbled bottom of a whisky glass, but best
of all was when we broke rocks on the surface with a rippled
water glass, blew it to bits,
making a diamond of stars, bright
as birth marks, that stretched across the whole night.
Meanwhile Ann-Marie was shouting at us

saying *put that away, your mum'll kill you,*
and *don't!* - or so I'd imagine, we were too busy.
All I know is that by the time
my mum set the council free and came home
Ann-Marie was crying saying what terrible
children we were and how she's never come near us again.

First Offence

My mother tells it like this:
there we were, posh outdoor
cafe; you, me, your dad,
you were one and all sticky
from the fair. This man was sat
at the next table; linen suit,
nice hands, eating a salad
topped off with a huge tomato.
You reached across, before we could stop
you and took it, bit in. He smiled.
I wanted the ground to open.

Here's what I remember:
reaching as far as I can to touch skin,
it's the colour of sweet, fresh cuts, wet paint,
wet, the place where tongues begin.
It smells of cool, grasslands,
silver pencils, never being thirsty again.
The rest is a haze, pale blue,, and getting
paler as only what matters travels
again and again from the eyes' lens
to the part of the brain that stores light
as memory. The reach of my hand.
The red of it. That tomato
was rightfully mine.

The Storm

Where were you the day the fish fell,
the day roads grew scales and every step
you took crunched although you tried to be careful?

We were walking through the park behind
our flats. It was alive - just -
with small fish the size of whitebait writhing

in the heat of their drying puddles. The next day
it happened again, but with bigger fish;
perch, catfish, red and blue Japanese

fighting fish. This time the fall was localised
to the football pitch. Then, two
weeks later came the periwinkles, which fell

only an hour before the lightning struck.
That was before the divers showed up,
in full rubber, dangling witnesses from branches

of street trees. By the end of the month we could clearly
see, high up on the sides of buildings
and moving higher, unmistakable ripples.

ken steedman
Hull, England

In An Empty House

Rain singing outside
and the porch a welcome shelter
for some passers by.

At the foot of the stairs
in half-light
I listen to their fluency
in a distant tongue
and feel privileged
on behalf of the house.

The radio reminds me of this later
as I turn through static
catching words
from beyond the curve of the earth.

Bridge

A north-east wind
tears free one end
of the banner
spanning our street
a railway bridge painted
in finest realist style.

Drawn by the wild clatter of canvas
against bricks
I hang from the bedroom window
disappointed
by my first clear view of the houses beyond.

Later
the silent rolling of stock past my window
tells me the rails have also broken free
and writhing sent
a slow train into the sky.

daithidh maceochaidh
York, England

Schrödinger's Cat

She never liked me,
mi mate's mum,
ever since the time
she found me
closing the door
on her cat –
microwave door that is.

That was it for me
with her
and perhaps
the cat too,
no matter that
I was only,
joking.

Later,
after that time
they took me in
after finding me
in the park
glued out of mi head
cutting mi wrists
with chance found bits
of broken glass,
she said, "Told you so –
bad 'un, that 'un."
This she said to mi mate,
her son,
still stroking her cat,
minus a life or two.

Black Kettle

Some now, any just
this moment,
alarm clock eventually
has its two-beeps worth,
as allus, the temptation,
not to sleep on,
but to moulder longer
into morning.

Shower hesitates atween
scolding and freezing,
notice cracks, yonder
plaster, check over
testicles, nothing wrong,
nothing more,
rinse off.

Pat dry with that red towel, should've gone
to the laundrette last week,
feel bark of skin on left-wrist,
fleet fancy to add yet
another year for auld time's sake.

In the parlour, Grandfather's
Carriage Clock, breaks seconds,
break wind, laugh like a child,
a girt gormless bairn again,
push back the curtain,
comb down hair, making best
job of it: *a windy day
is not for thatching.*

Time for a cuppa, a brew,
perhaps a rich tea or three,
hear next door's kids gan off
to school, milk-bottle kicked
skittles by backyard – bastards!
Sip tea.

Yon white tabby over t' road,
waint come in today.
Postman pushes through
letters for the last tenants,
put aside, wait for a rainy day.

Flick and thumb through
The Radio Times, searching
for something better though
'wireless is stuck on 3,
but it never hurts to look,
to ken, for once what one
is missing.

Put the kettle on,
time for another brew,
breath in –
breath out –
day in -
day out –
simple things
get hard.

The Man who Mistook his Wife for a Twat

They showed him all the snap-shots
of his wife as a tiny tot
bucket, spade, sunglasses
the whole job lot.

They showed him the X-ray photographs
of broken bones: ribs, wrists,
they even kept a couple of the old
signed plaster-casts.

There were the police reports,
marriage licence and her signature
on the mortgage contract
of that two-up/two down in Pontefract.

Much more than this was shown,
but they couldn't pull the wool over his eyes
they couldn't disguise the fact
that he mistook his wife for a twat.

In all other ways he was just a normal gaje,
liked football, curries, and copious beers
with the lads from the factory,
just his life with his wife was a mystery.

In all of forty years of marriage
for richer, for poorer, in sickness and in health
he'd never taken his Mrs for anything other than a garage
to park his prick, his fist, his fascination for human bondage.

And in the end
after all the tests were in
they never could find
anything wrong with him.

stephen wade

Scunthorpe, England

The President's Man

'Get your fucking face outta my life you prick!'
 That's the way he talks to me. And him almost a President. The President of this state. He has had no formal education as such, and these days a man may rise to a position of some eminence and have no letters, nor any culture. Hence my position here. As he constantly reminds me.
 'What do I pay ya for? Giving me some fucking culture, not cleaning teeth for God's sake.' He held his mouth like a child at the dentist, looking for sympathy from some bystanders. He has been in one of his moods all day. Constantly slapping one's backside, purposely swearing and being coarse, making remarks about my sexual tastes, and even undermining my official mentorship. He scoffs at the word. But I took him on today. I don't usually, but this afternoon he went too far.
 The overgrown ninny thinks you can buy culture at the corner shop, in a tube, apply it to your testicles and procreate great monsters of paintings and poems and sculptures.
 I had finally helped him wash and dress, managed to fasten his trousers around that vast gut of 48 inches, and reminded him that today was his Spanish lesson and his dialogue in cultural history. Then he insisted on eating sausages and watching some horrendous cartoon, so I turned it off and stared him in the eyes.
'What? What did you just do, Willis?' I could see sausage as he spoke. Some of it spewed out onto his dog, Plato, who ate it with relish.
'I turned that awful trash off, your Excellency.'
'But, but, I'm the President in two months. I'll be twenty one and you can fuck off.'
'Of course you are, but I'm your mentor, appointed by the Advisory Council. You will recall that my task is to shape you up by Christmas for the Summit.'
'Oh the pissing Summit... why did I agree to that? Okay, what's the timetable today, misery guts?'
 'Spanish... then dinner etiquette. There are times when I

wonder how you came to be Alfred Bewar's son. Alfred had it all – charm, manners, a degree, charisma... ' I reminded him that his father had arrived a mere adventurer and created a nation state. 'Shut it you British prick, or I'll sack you.' He stamped the floor like a little boy in primary school. I reminded him that I could only be sacked by the Advisory Council. His response was to start taking his suit off. 'I want to wear jeans and my baggy top. I want to play soccer. You're British – you know soccer. That's culture. You promised to teach me soccer – last week you promised, you prick.'

His chubby body looked bizarre, shaking there before the fireplace in that vast mansion. His black hair was plastered down with glossy cream, and his red flesh wobbled on that over-indulgent face. He is thirty one but looks like a teenager, overfed and neglected. 'I mean, you used to play for that team right – Blackburn Rovers. Some frigging top team over there?'
'I had a trial for them, Excellency.'
'Okay. Look, if I do some Spanish, will you teach me how to do a banana kick?'

I agreed. I also agreed to his wearing casual clothes. Anything to get some teaching done. He kept mumbling, *I want a fuck... I need a fuck. Haven't been laid in a month.* I noticed there was a chocolate stain on his top. That was too much. 'Stop! Shirt off at once. Mrs. Sturt... MRS. STURT!' I called out across the wood-panelled room. She was there promptly, that wonderful woman, and in seconds, the shirt was taken to be washed and a clean one sent for.
'Now, Excellency... *Buenas dias. Que tal?*'
'Huh? Oh fuck... *Que fuckin tal.*'
I sighed. '*Senor, donde puedo comprar vino tinto?*'
'Er, just a minute. *Un momento senor...* ' He made a gurgling noise and struggled to find a word. I decided to encourage him. 'Bravo Excellency... you spoke Spanish well there. Well done indeed.'
'I did? So now some soccer?'

I had to agree. After all, he needed to shed some pounds. He was a pudding with power and today he needed to shrink a little.

freckled. We both changed into shorts and Brazil tops in his personal gym. He was hairy and freckled almost everywhere. The beard he was trying to grow had reached that awful patchy, blotchy stage. He also has a perspiration problem. Perhaps that is all down to his habit of wolfing down junk food and endlessly watching poorly made sensational films.
'Now... you're an old guy... how old are you now Willis?' He asked as we jogged out into his personal five-a-side pitch.
'Fifty three Excellency.'
'Christ! You wanna start watching all the TV adverts in the afternoon – you know, life insurance, stairlifts, all that shit. I'll buy you a stairlift if you like.' He chuckled and pounded his blubbery frame over to the middle of the gym. 'Okay. Here's a ball. Now I got this gardener guy in the goal. Show me how to do a free kick that bends into the top corner.'
'Hello Carlos!' I waved to the gardener who was in the goals, standing there like a spare part, with no idea what a goalkeeper has to do. He was over sixty anyway, with only one fully-operational leg.

I tried to show him a straight driven shot, and then how to curve the foot around the ball and so on. He thought he had it. He smiled. Then he cracked the ball with his toe-end, and by good fortune it went straight at Carlos like an arrow and hit him in the belly. He keeled over in pain. I went to help, and called for Mrs. Sturt.

Really, I could have put one on his chin, Our Excellency. He had about thirty balls lined up, and various minions passed them to him one by one. Time after time he cracked the shots well wide, or he hit the gym ceiling. He was turning red with anger and frustration,
'I can't fucking do it... you're a crap teacher Willis. You British are shit at this game. I want a Brazilian cultural mentor. You're an old piss-artist. Go find a fucking grave and lie in in... and get out GET OUT YOU SCUM' He screamed at the assembled lackeys, who were all glad to escape and sprinted out into the sunshine back to their normal duties.

He sat on the hard floor and cursed everything. There was sweat on the floor around him, as if some horrible slug had

slithered across. 'I need a fuck. I'm better at screwing than this shit.'
'Well you are not to have any female company. Not until we have done dinner etiquette. We have a syllabus to follow, Excellency.'

He made mock-polite comments about my appearance. He noted my bald head, my false teeth and my small build. He also took exception to my rather smart black coat and pin-striped trousers. I explained that I had been trained as a gentleman's gentleman, and that I was also at one time a professional tailor. Once again, I reminded him that I had been born into a miner's family in Yorkshire, in the North of England, and that culture and education had helped me up in the world.
'Yorkshire? That where all the soot is and the guys with flat caps right?'
'You must begin to understand the world in ways other than through Hollywood film and ridiculous comic-strips.' I scalded him.
I shower, then we'll get to it. We have dinner, and I'll show you where to put all the knives and stuff yeah? But I'll tell you one thing – I'm gonna hit a penalty shot past you by Christmas, and that's fact!'

He washed, and I thanked God for some respite from him. I had a coffee and stared at the lawns for a while. Even then I heard his manic singing from the shower. The only song he knew by heart was *La Bamba* as that had been our first Spanish lesson.

Then, just before lunch, I went to check on the girl. She was sitting in the hallway, her head down. All silent and alone. Behind her stood the two drivers who did the collecting for His Excellency's hobbies.
I asked who she was.
'*Es una chica – lindo....mucho lindo.*' One of the collectors said. She looked up at me and I saw this very young, pure face. She must have been sixteen at the most. Unwashed but somehow very pure. '*Me llamo Teresa.*'

I put my fingers under her chin, and lowered my face to hers. Looking into those deep, paradisal eyes, I decided that this time he was not going to have her.
She pulled away and tugged her blue jacket tight to her bodice.
'You are too good for this job, little one. She is too young.' I said, looking accusingly at the drivers. They told me his Excellency would not be too happy without some fanny. But I said I would take the blame and off they went, with the girl in tow.
'No... no, let the girl stay. She can have something to eat.'
'Of course. Something to eat...' One of them leered at me.
I heard one of them mutter something about 'a screw is a screw' as he walked into the shade of the foyer.

Well, we made a little progress today. The oaf learned a new word – simply because it was an obscenity – and as his sexual tension had not been relieved by the young visitor yesterday he was not in a pliant mood and certainly eager to curse and let a fist fly.
'You go on about Alfred Bewar my dear father. Point is, I never knew him, old man. No, like you, he was of that generation of gentlemen who watched cricket and were polite to the ladies, yes? No-one is called Willis and Alfred any more. You both belong to the past. You belong to Death. Anyway, I want to play computer games today, You can go to the cafe and play chess with your cronies.'
'Ah no, I tell you what – we make a deal. You do some lessons this morning, and I'll go to the cafe after lunch.'
He agreed, and we settled down to art and the history of painting. I set up my slides. He fidgeted and sucked sweets in the semi-darkness.
'Okay, now today we're looking at Hogarth, the great English satirical artist of the eighteenth century... this is his famous *Gin Lane*...'
'Oh Christ!'
'Now, your Excellency, may I remind you that the Advisory Council are coming in two days to check on our progress? If you're not clearly a more rounded individual then...'
'Then they'll sack your sad old ass!' He laughed manically.
I walked across to where he sat. There was a stain growing on

the seat.
'Look, you made me pee myself, Willis old dear!'

Today I was able to take a day off. The officers from the Advisory Council escorted his Monstership to the races. The idea is to train him as a good host. Visitors will most definitely want to see the races. Next to the bullfight, it's the cultural; highlight of the social calendar. But I collected my mail – and there was this note from the President: 'Four weeks – then I hit that shot past you. I been practising!'

This seems to be growing into some kind of vendetta. Next it will be graffiti and annoying phone calls – a war of the mind, the nerves. Well, if that's what he wants, then he's against the absolute master.

I took the opportunity to amble across the plaza to see the lads and play some chess or dominoes talk politics and books, and recall better times. What else is there when you're almost at the stage when the sawbones start taking bits of you away? There's Manuel, a real old gentleman with a ranch of his own, and Peter who teaches English at the college here.

We sipped some wine and left the dominoes for a while because Peter was in one of his querulous moods. He was fat and pink-fleshed, with the usual shiny grey Italian suit. He brushed his elegant wooden cane across his well-glossed brogues as he lamented the standards falling.

'The young... ah, I despair! No sense of grammar, no notion of how to use a colon – and worse, no political sense. Do you know, I asked them yesterday what their opinion of the Third World Debt was, and one young man said it was all about lazy bastards in India who didn't do a day's work. I mean, I've got kids who think the Jews brought the Holocaust on themselves!'

I commented that they did not read, but Manuel went a little further.

'No, see... in this country, and in all South America, the young, they see Yanks and they see movies, and sex, all this – they want the same, only now. No manana for them.'

I did a lot of listening. It was hot. By four, I left to lie down and dream of England. It happens more often now – I think of

Leeds all those years ago. I left in 1969. My God, what a year to be young! But strangely, I think not of the Beatles and drugs and Radio Caroline. No, I dwell on Jane, the girl I should have married. Here I am, an old bachelor, and my destiny was to be happy with her. Destinies can be defeated by circumstance, I think... She spoke softly. We played ten-pin bowling; we kissed in bus-shelters; we watched Bond films together. We sat in the rain and talked rebellion – against all the damned suburbs and the rules that made us struggle to find somewhere to lie down together.

I looked in the mirror before bedtime and wondered who that was, the old man with the ghost of a beard and creases webbing his face like netting. Willis Taylor, that's who. Born Leeds, 1945 in the heat of victory. Love in the streets. Yes, born in a time of carnival and brought up in a gallery of miserable faces. Willis Taylor, five feet six in his socks, an inner exile and a foreigner here. But also Willis Taylor, gentleman – a guy who had picked up two degrees and six languages, served in the navy, the police and the diplomatic service.

And now, he was a guy being challenged to a penalty shot by some brainless spoilt kid. Why isn't the guy a don, a managing director or something? Fuck me. No idea.

In fact, as I walked out to stare at the moon with a glass of red wine nestled in my hand, I was not too sure who I was. But I still have plans. Who doesn't? I'll be making plans in the condemned cell. I'll be thinking of Jane as well. Ash-blonde hair, slight as a ballet-dancer, soft voice, gentle touch. Words that caressed your spirit. Always had a sad and gentle smile, an understanding about everything. Jane Barugh, mysterious European. No-one ever knew where her family came from.

Then the old rover slept, soaked with red wine and daft sentiments.

This was a major bastard day. And it's November already. I mean, I have to do a Professor Higgins on this neanderthal by Christmas, when he is to emerge as the complete gentleman who will show the world how modern and powerful this country is. If I do it, I shall demand a large pension and an estate in the tranquil northern provinces.

He wanted a day off and nothing was going to deny him. He walked into our study after breakfast and immediately spat on my best rug. I wanted to crack him across the face. Somehow I gathered some poise and walked over to him, looked him in the eyes and demanded that he sat down and told me about Dickens. I had given him *Great Expectations* to read.
'How far have you got your Excellency?'
'Ah, to the part where the sister gets brutal. She's a bitch. I hate the book. It's like, for kids.'
'But it's a classic and you should know the best work by the best minds.'
'Well there is a problem Willis old chap – it's boring! I mean, if this guy is one of the best minds, what's a schmuck at the bottom of the place gonna be like? Some dork!' 'You want to be a dork? Hey? You will be if you persist with this attitude. Now, if you read the first four chapters by tomorrow, you can have some time with a... a young lady.'

That was desperation – always my last resort. But amazingly, he wanted something else.
'Na... soccer. I want you to teach me how to play like Gazza – so I can beat you old man!'
'Gazza? How can I do that?'
'You're fucking Willis Taylor, you know everything.' He sniggered and started sucking on an unlit cigarette.

I agreed. Anything to tire him out. And he would tire before me. The blubber would see to that. In fact, I was determined to bring him down. I was tired of all his bullshit and I was going to drive a shot in and frighten his little aristo heart.

So again there we were in the gym. He was hopeless really. No balance, no finesse, no sense of weighting a pass. He simply walloped the ball as hard as possible every time it came near him. But this time there was something different.
I became aware of a noise in a corner of the immense building, and suddenly there was a giant screen, showing Gazza's amazing goal against Scotland at Wembley. Some of his Excellency's friends were up there and they were showing the goal over and over again.

'See... now that is the kind of culture I want to learn, Willis. Get going, old man!'

There was a chorus of laughter from up in the top tiers of the gym. I was going to humiliate his Excellency. Either that, or he would become a footballer, and then maybe I could win something against this monstrous tide of barbarism in this God-forsaken place.

A man can dream, can't he?

'In goal, now Willis. I'm going to smack a shot past you.'

The crowd of druggies and alcos in the gallery cheered and shouted at me. 'Old bastard' they said. 'Knackered old Brit pimp.' That sort of thing.

I stood in the middle of the goal and jumped up and down. It was easy. I just had to watch his eyes. He had no idea of the psychology involved. He'd probably toe-end it wide, anyway. The fool pranced around and leered at his mates, who were louder and louder. One of them turned on a ghetto-blaster right behind the goal. It hit me behind like an on-coming train, but though my heart jumped, I showed no response. Just spat on my gloves and stared at tubby as he ran up to the ball.

I could see by his foot and his eyes that it was a side-foot to the left, and I went a shade early, just to be sure. The ball came right at my midriff. No problem. I curled around it and let the gratifying drop into silence take its course.

'Fuck! You old twat! Lucky or what?' He kicked at the floor. His mates were grumbling, but clearly impressed.

'Now, Mr. President, I'll take a penalty against you. How about if I score, you do the Spanish homework and the etiquette exercises before dinner?'

'Deal'

The audience stamped approval. We changed places. He smiled at me pitiably. But I knew he was scared. He was in for a shock, and he sensed trouble. He took his place on the line and sort of lurched forward, then slapped his gloved hands together. I put the ball down on the spot and prepared to crack a drive right at him. HE would move out of the way,

I was sure. If he didn't then he might stop the shot but...

I took care to step up and belt the thing smack in the middle, right at him, like a bolt. As I hit the ball, the loud mob above screamed at me and something was thrown towards me – a snooker ball I think. But the ball went screaming just to his head, and in defence, he stuck a hand up. The ball smashed into the net and he went down, yelling in pain.

Several attendants rushed to him, and before I could have a look, a doctor was holding the blubbery fool's hand. 'Dislocated finger, your Excellency. I'll put it back. Just look away.'

There was a click and the kid cried out in pain. The crowd moved away as he stood up. 'I'll get you, Willis. I'll see you dead for this!' He ran away to his rooms. Everyone looked at me. It was hard not to chuckle to myself.

December first, and the world wants Christmas to start now. Well, I don't care what else, I must stop this dreaming about Jane. A fatal mistake has been made. I wrote about her in my diary, and I'm afraid it's led to an unwelcome situation. His Excellency (now making a little progress in etiquette) has yet to learn that privacy is important to people. Yes – he looked at a few pages as I was at the toilet. I left him writing some sort of letter – a diplomacy thing – and when I came back, he smiled and said, 'Oh, how sweet. You loved this girl Jane?'
So we had one of our periodic conversations about women and sex. It is always the same with him. He demolishes everything to animal urges. I could slap him in that mood.
'So, it was romantic with this girl. You English love to be coy?'
'It was romantic, but you wouldn't understand. We enjoyed each other's company.
We talked, we dined, we went to the cinema..'
'Ah yes, fucking on the back seat yes? My father was American, but he talked of this.'
'No. We didn't, I mean we never...'

That's what I said. Oh my God, why did I say it. That little word *never* could sink me. His face lit up as if he had witnessed the parting of the Red Sea. Then his smile – it was like the rising of a black sun.

'So you had this young lady... let me get this right... and you wined her and you dined her but you never screwed her? Right?'

I walked about the room. He had found a weak spot. How could I explain? I tried. I talked about deep love and respect; about getting to know the other. All that. But his smile would not go. That leering, that triumph of the schoolboy over Sir. Sir was stupid. Sir probably watched *Brief Encounter* and sobbed at tear-jerkers in his sad little room.
Or, was Sir... was Sir *gay?*

Yes, we had it all through December until this fatal date of the 20th when we have to test His Excellency on his knowledge. I kept finding little notes addressed to Ms Willis. Once he bought me a dress. I just laughed it off.

Oh yes, but I'm going to sort out the little swine. He's going to fail, and I don't care if it ruins me. Today we rehearsed.
I sat him in an armchair in the library and gave him the spiel.
'Your Excellency. Today we test out all the results of our hard work. You are dressed in a beautiful Italian suit. You have washed, applied moisturising creams, polished the shoes, practised the right smile. We have a few days left, but I feel that we have succeeded. Thank you for your efforts. Now you will proceed next door where you will have dinner with a select group of ministers. During this meal, you will be filmed and recorded. In the process of the eight courses, you will have to do the following:
1. Speak Spanish to people who address you in that tongue.
2. Handle the protocol properly.
3. Avoid all obscenities in your speech.
4. Give a talk to the group on your subject – now are we keeping to the one you have learned?
  He yawned. 'Yes, fucking trade relations with Peru.'
'Last week you knew it by heart. Have you got it firmly in there now?' I rapped his head.
'Yes my dear. Have you a kiss for me?'
I wanted to slap him but restrained myself. He nodded.
  So we went ahead and he did very well. He swore twice and he spilt some soup down his tuxedo. His Spanish never went

115

beyond *'Hola, como se llama.?'* but all this
is progress. We are dealing here with a brute, you recall.

So, it's the night after the big day. People celebrated all over Cafelia. Fireworks. Parties. The young blubber passed his tests and is to be sworn in tomorrow. He did just the same as in the rehearsal – only this time he forgot the last section of his speech. No-one noticed, as they were all drunk. I have succeeded in making a sort of robot who does about twenty 'cultural' things and then runs off to screw a whore and berate his Maker. And what have I done? I'll tell you. I played football.

I played football because I want to live here. To play chess, to read the literary weeklies. Yes, even to dream about Jane and to look at her photograph in my wallet, dwelling on everything she means to me and what I live for.

The fat boy lumbered up and toe-ended the ball. It swerved a bit, but I had it covered. Then I slipped, patted the ball but only into the net, and I rolled over, eating the dust in defeat. The ghetto-blaster went to full volume and the voice of His Excellency said, from somewhere above me as I faked exhaustion: 'See, I said I'd stick one past you old man! ' He ruffled my thinning hair and ran across to his adoring pals.

So I kept a nice little job of Educational Chairman in that favourite little committee that the Advisory Council loves so much. All I have to do is say a few words like *book, text, ideology* and so on. The foreign guests like me and I let them beat me at chess. Alfred Bewar would forgive me. He was one of my lot.

carol coiffait
Welton, England

Reginald Dixon Is Alive And Well In Lincolnshire

Hand in hand under the stars
we walk our dog. Orion
and his dog stroll along too
southwards to the river.

We want to see the biggest
organ in the world, played by
Reg Dixon. He's given up
Blackpool and the BBC
and only does the winter
season in South Ferriby.

See, that's him, just to the left
of that last tree. He's taking
a bow, to wild applause
he is adjusting his cuffs
and flicking his coat-tails, he sits
hands raised, ready to play...

His signature tune thunders
over the Humber: "Oh I
Do like to be Beside the
Seaside." His next number
is "Winter Wonderland"
Then "All through the Night" he plays
the old tunes that we love to hear

Till it is time for his swan-song:
"Moonlight and Roses". Then, as the dawn
appears, Reg and the organ slowly sink
into the mud.

Drosophila - Feral Male/Female

I am Amanda. Hazel eyes, auburn hair...
I AM Amanda, so don`t be calling me Terry any more.
Oh, I'll still wear the Forty Shades of Green:- Fine wool suits,
suede coats and as silk under-kegs; all I am prepared to do
is pad a little, here and here, shave my legs and maybe eat less spuds.

Who SAYS I should wear make-up?
I know plenty girls who don`t and they`re just fine - OK?
You can tell who the Hell you like in this old town.
Aye, and your Granny. I'm leaving for London,
Paris or maybe New York even.

And why, in God's name, do you think I'd need a fanny?
I've told you Kat, I think sex is a dirty game.
It's high time the body became a temple again,
not so much Catholic or Proddy muck to be shot at
or otherwise fucked by any man with a stomach for it.

Of course I'll write. You know I'll always love you Kat,
but I can't hang around here. No, the Home's not so bad
and it's getting better inside my head
now I've made up my mind to run. Och, don`t cry.
What fun? There's not been much of that now has there?

How can you say that Kat, to me your brother?
Save it for our long-lost Mother.
Tell her, if you ever see her, that you have a SISTER
not a BROTHER. A traveller, a rolling stone like our Da,
the feral old arse that caused all the pain in our bloody story.

Now kiss me. There there. And don`t worry, it'll be all right.
I'll let you know where I get to. And yes! I said I'd write.
Now go on up...Goodnight.

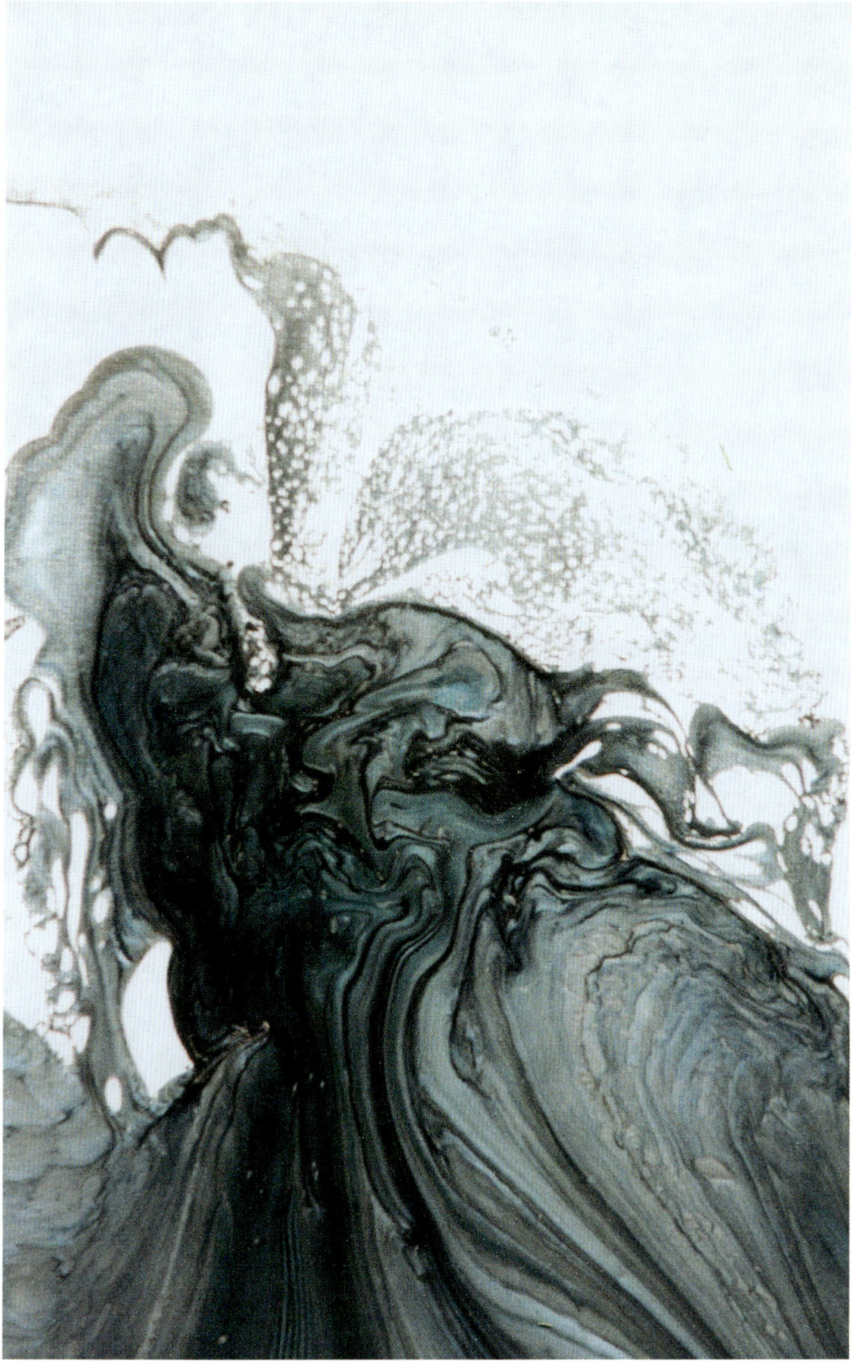

ben myers
London, England

Box-Star Bobby

Bobby walked straight up to the counter.
"I'd like to buy a cunt please,"
"Excuse me?" said the assistant looking up from her clipboard. She was young, in her early twenties, a possible student.
"I'd like to buy a cunt please."
"Could you be a little more specific please? This is, after all, a cunt shop," she said, making no effort to disguise her impatience. "What type would you like?"
"What types do you have?" asked Bobby.
"Well, we currently stock the standard traditional 50s model, the SF-Super Sixty Deluxe which comes in a choice of colours, the new sleek hand-held cunt which is imported from Japan" –she paused, looking at Bobby", - that one costs a little more than average. We also have the Deep Pink which comes with an air-conditioning option, the Hairy French Maid, the Cave Of Borneo, the detachable Red Snapper, the Three-Fold Eurohole, the All New Three-Fold Eurohole, the Latin Satin, the XL Polygrip Supreme, all of the Vaj Elite series, plus the Clam, the Aphrodite and the Venus Man-Trap."
"Wow," said Bobby, scratching his three-day stubble. "I didn't know that there were so many cunts on the market."
"You'd be surprised," said the assistant. "I think we've still got some Fudge Tunnels back there too if you're interested."
"Oh no," said Bobby, taking a step backwards. "A cunt will be fine."
"Then of course there's sizes."
"Shoot," said Bobby. "I never thought of that."
The assistant looked over the top of her steel-rimmed spectacles.
"Looking at you now, I'd say that a six-by-two would suffice."
"You can tell just by looking at me?"
"Sir," said the assistant curtly. "I'm a trained professional. However, it is best to double-check."

"OK," said Bobby.
"Would you mind?"
Bobby cleared his throat and then unzipped his fly and laid his meat on the counter.
"If you could take two steps to your left please," said the assistant. Bobby slid his cock along the smooth counter. She tugged it gently until it lined up beside an intricate looking device that was a cross between a ruler and a spirit level, but which also had a small digital screen and a number of buttons running along it.
"Do you needs my balls?" said Bobby.
"No sir, this will do just fine."
While she took his measurements, Bobby sighed deeply and looked around the shop at the colourful displays and the pickling jars on the shelves, the bright strip lights that ran the length of the ceiling, the magazine rack, the diagrams, the accessories and the broken cunts stacked up behind the repairs counter until his eyes met with a harness hanging from the ceiling in the corner of the shop, encased in a small perspex booth.
"What's that for?" asked Bobby.
"Installation," said the girl without looking up from his cock, which she'd stretched out like a snakeskin before him.
"Cool."
"But that costs extra."
"That's alright," said Bobby cheerfully. "It wouldn't be permanent anyway. I just thought that it was time that I had one around the house."
"76.4% of our customers buy their cunts from us for the very same reason," she replied. "Now, have you settled on a model?"
"Yeah," said Bobby. "I think I'll go for a detachable Red Snapper."
"Good choice. What colour?"
"What colour?" said Bobby. "Jeez, well now, I think I'll have it in...blue?"
The shop assistant picked up a small microphone from the counter.

"One Red Snapper in blue," she said, her voice monotone over the public address system. "Standard size, twenty degree rotation on the head shaft. No leeway."
"Excuse me," said Bobby. "But what does that mean?"
"It's just standard stuff, sir."
Bobby looked at her in her starched white lab coat, hair tied in a bun, sturdy glasses, razorblade mouth.
"Right."
"And how would you like to pay? We have an excellent hire purchase scheme with a one-year guarantee on all new brands. We take all major credit cards including Astro, Milk-It, Blackmail Express and Big Daddy-O, and we operate a part exchange service on worn, out of line cunts."
"Cash is fine," said Bobby.
"Cash," she inexplicably said into the microphone.
While Bobby paid, a similar looking assistant appeared from the back of the shop with a brown cardboard box in her hand. She put in on the counter.
"One Red Snapper in blue, standard, twenty degree rotation on the head shaft, with free non-durable waist clips."
Bobby nodded.
"There's a special on at the moment," she replied by way of explanation, and then disappeared into the back of the shop.
"Gift wrapped?" asked the first assistant.
"What?" said Bobby. "Oh no. No thank you."
She put the box with the cunt in it into a carrier bag and passed it over the counter to Bobby, her face blank and lifeless.
"Enjoy your cunt," she said.
"I will," said Bobby. "And thank you."
He left the shop closing the door behind him and wandered the car park until he found his car. Then he started up the engine, wound down the window, turned the radio on and looked at the cunt in the box beside him. He jammed the gear stick into first and pulled away quickly.

The Turnbuckle Larceny

Turnbuckle was attempting to dissolve two aspirin in a plastic cup into which he'd added a thumb of water from the cooler when the phone rang. He swirled the cloudy mixture around watching the little pills decrease in size, small plumes of white powder rising from them and swaying in the water like anemones in the tide. It was too early and he was too new to the job to hate it as much as he did. Still, from small acorns grow large salaries. Six months more of pen pushing and he'd review his options. He was fast track. He'd move up, that much he was certain.
Turnbuckle put the cup aside, took a deep breath to clear his head and picked up the phone on the seventh ring.
"Hello, Metropolitan Police force," he said, noting the ease at which his pre-programmed greeting fell out of his mouth like a cold piece of metal that he'd been choking on. The Supe would be proud of his telephone manner. Public relations in the Met, had not been going so well recently. "Officer Turnbuckle speaking, how may I help you?"
"Hll? Hll?," said the voice at the other end. "Cn y hr m?"
"Yes sir, loud and clear," replied Turnbuckle as he plucked a biro from his desk tidy and turned to a fresh page of his logbook. "What appears to be the problem?"
"Wll, yr nt gng t blv ths, bt sm tght bstrd hs stln ll my vwls. Jst lk tht – gn!"
"Stolen your vowels? Wow. I can see that this misfortune has affected your speech somewhat. When were you last in possession of all five of your vowels, Mr -?"
"Mr Bckr. Lst nght. Thy wr stll thr lst nght whn lft th pb rnd clsng tm."
Turnbuckle gave the aspirin one last swill and then poured it down the back of his throat in one fluid movement, remembering the difficulty at which he had swallowing the bitter pills as a child.

"They were still there last night when who left the pub at closing time?" he asked, swallowing hard twice.
"M."
"M? Who's 'M'? Did he take the vowels?"
"N, m."
"Oh, you mean you. You should have said so."
" dd."
"Sorry?"
"Frgt t."
Turnbuckle glanced down at the logbook and the large unblinking eye that he had subconsciously penned, its long thick eyelashes shooting off across the page in all directions. He always got the nutters, the kook-jobs, he thought to himself as the eye stared back, but that was the way when you were on the bottom rung. Besides, the public relied on him and he relied on the job.
Everyone relies on someone.
"And are they valuable to you sir, these vowels?"
"F crs thy'r fckng vlble y gnrnt pg. M nly hlf th mn usd t b wtht thm."
"Excuse me sir, but you're going to have to speak a little bit slower, I'm afraid," Turnbuckle sighed, the faint thump behind eyes returning once again.
"Try taking some deep breaths if it helps, Mr-?"
"Bckr. Tld y my nm s Bckr."
"Of course you did," smiled Turnbuckle patronisingly into the phone.
He seemed to spend half his life speaking to these people as if they were five years old. One day he'd be macing wanted criminals in the face or finding cache cases full of uncut cocaine on random car searches, but for now he had to resign himself to being little more than a kindergarten teacher with too many hangovers.
"Sd, m hlf th mn usd t b," the voice said impatiently.
"Let me see: you're only half...the man...you used to be?"
His brain felt like it was floating in battery acid, an imaginary cold steel band being tightened around his skull,

133

yet Turnbuckle prided himself on his ability to read a situation and offer an immediate diagnosis. He was, he felt, a problem solver for the people. His stomach lurched, reminding him that a Met police officer must not only be vigilant but fed, groomed and fit and ready for action at all times. He'd never make CID if he kept skipping breakfast.
"Ys, ys! Tht's rght!"
"I thought that's what you said," he mumbled. "Right, well, I'll get one of my officers onto the case. Let me see, Officer Saxby has a lot of experience in the field...it was he who effectively solved the sound laundering case a couple of years back."
"Snd lndrng?"
"Oh yes sir, I'm surprised you didn't here about it – it was all over the papers at the time. Officer Saxby was personally commended by the commissioner for his work on the case. He managed to infiltrate a ring of known criminals who had a lucrative operation laundering sounds back into the system They had a network of gophers who were stealing various sounds – car horns, sirens, kids shouting and so forth – and then selling them on at a price to the bosses who, in turn, surreptitiously released them back onto the streets. They were clever, I'll give them that much, but not clever enough for The Met unfortunately. They're all incarcerated now, serving between one and three years each. As far as we understand, all sounds on the street now belong to their rightful owners."
" s," said the caller, clearly unimpressed with the case that Turnbuckle had relayed to him as an example of the efficiency and success rate of today's inner city policing.
"What?"
"Nvmnd," said the caller impatiently.
Turnbuckle glanced at his standard issue wristwatch and remembered the day he qualified and the aspirations and expectations that came with the miniature warfare package of handcuffs, extendable truncheon and so forth with which he was presented. Eighteen months seemed like a long time

when you were chained to a desk and their was drug epidemic in the city, not to mention thieves left, right and centre.
It was 11.13am. That left six hours and forty-seven minutes until he could go home. He made another quick calculation: four hundred and seven minutes. Twenty-four thousand, four hundred and twenty seconds.
"Hll? Hll?" said the caller impatiently, his tones distorted and misshapen by his recent impediment. It sounded like he was talking with two sets of teeth and the line was cutting out intermittently. It sounded like he had a mouthful of marbles. Turnbuckle smiled to himself.
"Well, anyway," he said, suddenly remembering that it was his turn to speak. "In the meantime I'll pop some lost property forms in the post for you right away. Now, if you could just tell me your address."
"K 'ts: Wdwd Rd, Cmbrwll, Lndn, S JH."
"You'll have to give me the house number first, sir."
"Sd 'ts Wdwd Rd..."
"Nope," said Turnbuckle sitting back in his chair and twirling his set of cuffs around a finger until they careered off the tip, clattering across the desk towards his cooling cup of coffee. "All I'm getting is bizarre kind of croaking noise here. Now - slower this time - what number house do you live at?"
" ."
"Still nothing there sir."
"Sht, sht sht," growled the caller. "Thy'v stln th nmbrs aswll, th drty rottn pcs f sht! 'll kll thm whn gt my hnds n th thvng mgrls!"
He hung up.
Turnbuckle tore the page from his logbook, screwed up the etching of the eye, threw it into the wastebasket and reached for the bottle of aspirin again. There was four hundred and six minutes until he finished. That, Turnbuckle calculated, worked out at twenty-four thousand, three hundred and sixty seconds.
He began to count out loud as he reached for his coffee.

"Twenty-four thousand, three hundred and fifty-nine... twenty-four thousand, three hundred and fifty-eight..." The phone rang again, but this time he ignored it. "Twenty-four thousand, three hundred and fifty-seven..."

You Are The Gallery

The back room of the chemist was poorly lit and the air conditioning had long since sighed its last carcinogenic breath and gone to a better place. A place where air conditioners ruled the land as masters and portable heaters were their loyal servants. Sam thought about these things. He thought about them too much.

But now the room was stuffy and claustrophobic with its sepia lighting that threatened to slowly push you into a coma. Just thinking about another day beneath the hot table lamp made Sam's chest tighten and his back ooze ice-cold droplets of sweat. One brief thought of the room could ruin whole weekends. Sometime, during sex, he'd see the piles of envelopes and hear the distant digital tinkle of the bell. The image would inspire the blood to withdraw from his hard-on leaving him angry and empty as she closed her eyes and undoubtedly fantasised about someone taller and stronger from her well-ventilated, well lit office.

The back room of the chemist was a slow killer.

Sam developed pictures for a living. You took him your film and he gave you hard copy snapshots so that you could conserve your memory for important things like shopping lists, birthdays, useless statistics and death. Sometimes he could do it in less than an hour. That cost more.

For Sam the magic within the process had long since disappeared. Maybe if he could breath in some fresh air once in a while he might find something of worth within the job. Failing that, he could at least tolerate it and therefore avoid clouding his life with thoughts of pestilence, extreme violence, the countryside, credit cards, knives, fresh air and shit. But as long as the bare bulb feebly bathed the room in thick slabs of brown and he fed another reel into the cantankerous farting machine, Sam was resigned to this piecemeal suicide.

So Sam started the project. It just happened by accident. He was packaging a 36-exposure ready for a collection when, without thinking, he thumbed his way through the first half dozen snaps. He hadn't looked at photographs in quite a while. He never took pictures because he doesn't want reminding of anything. He'd rather get drunk and fuck, but even that one pleasure was being depleted, corrupted, eroded. All he could do was get drunk and listen to his two records. And he never looked at the dozens of pictures that flopped out of the machine each day. Sam had never realised that so many people took so many photos in London. And London is just one city. Before the job he'd never really thought about it, but he'd still been surprised back then in his pharmacy salad days. It seemed like more people existed in photographs than in real life.

He didn't have a woman when he started at the chemists - he had loads of them. And now he had a good one but his body and mind were being separated as if they were polar-opposite magnet forces. They were repelled by each other all because of the job. It was killing him and the air conditioning had moved over to the other side. He couldn't think straight at work and at night his mind was cluttered with images that he didn't want to consider.

As Sam flicked through the barely dry batch he pulled out a close-up portrait of a young, beautiful girl, about sixteen years old with stylishly cropped brown hair. Her face had recently moved from child to young woman and she glowed with the energy and sex of post-pubescence. Her eyes were closed and she was laughing. The lighting was pretty good for a cheap camera with an amateur behind it.

Sam slipped the photo into the pocket of his black jeans so that it followed the contours of his thigh. He shoved the rest of the pictures into the packet, sealed it and put into the wire tray on the right hand side of his desk, under a drawing-pinned quote from Henry Miller that Sam could never remember word for word.

When the machine coughed out the next batch like a rough cough candy flavoured phlegm ball, Sam picked them up, walked out of the back room, down the short hall and out the side door into the alleyway. Fresh air, at last. He sat down, back against the wall, lit up a Silk Cut and started going through the pictures, studying them with more detail this time. It was family stuff, taken at a party somewhere tacky. Loads of half – pissed people too old to be cool, too stupid to go anywhere in life. Bad teeth and crap hair. Arms around each other. Dancing. Pretending.

Slotting the photos behind one another he stopped at one of a redhead: good cleavage, late thirties. Pretty sexy in an older woman-type way. The combination of looking at her and being stimulated by the long overdue nicotine and the fresh, fresh air gave him an erection. The rest of the pictures were just the usual shit. Whilst the red-haired stayed the others moved back to their owner and, in a mere three hours, would find themselves being passed around a kitchen table in over-priced flat in West London.

Sam threw the cigarette butt down the alley and went back inside, the transition from light to dark throwing turquoise shapes up into his vision as his eyes struggled to re-adjust. He wanted another cigarette.

The room was getting smaller.

And so it went on day after day, punctuated only by regular drinking binges, the constant use of marijuana and the mechanical sex down on the mattress. The photo collection, however, increased. In two weeks Sam brought home ten new friends, one each day; occasionally crumpled or creased from the too-packed tube ride home where his CD Walkman was the only salvation from the madness and murder and heat of the end of day stampede. But they still came faithfully by his side, frozen in states of spontaneity.

Each day Sam blue-tacked another addition to his wall. It felt

like Christmas, like advent, when each morning before school throughout December he would open another door to see another scene. Sometimes there was chocolate. Sometimes there wasn't. It reminded him of back then, in a twisted kind of way, Back then there were things to look
forward to, even if they usually were a let down the anticipation was as exciting as the event itself, whatever it may have been. Nothing was cool anymore. Especially the back room of the chemists. How could it be? Fresh air hadn't circulated in there for years. The most turbulence that that cave had seen was when a moth flapped its wings a good few months back.

At home Sam sometimes smoked a joint, naked from the waist up, cooling off and looking at the gallery of strangers.

At weekends the girl wanted to go out dancing but Sam hated clubs and the people with their bad chat-ups and perfume and shirts and fags and fights, all of them grasping at straws. Chasing something – anything. Lost, empty. He couldn't talk to her, only the basics: what they'd been doing. No mention of feelings or ambition, plans or ideas. So this was what is was going to be like. Early twenties and fucked.

That room.

He'd lie on the floor and look at the photos: pouting girls, an Asian in full robes, two hip young things with their arms round each – possible lesbians – a fat, miserable looking middle aged woman slumped in an equally miserable over-stuffed armchair, a student with her face obscured by a bottle of Becks, a youngster with bad skin and talking on a mobile, a Kate Winslett lookalike. He gave them names, created scenarios and tried not to think about the room and the fake digital tinkle that drilled into his head x amount of times per day so that it felt like every waking hour was spent with a constant hangover.

Sam hadn't written anything in ages and he liked to drink

vodka while looking out of his fifth storey window, listening to the sirens and watching the mental cases with their cans of beer, the shit stains on their shirt tails and their concealed knives. Sometimes he just looked down at the pavement until he went into a kind of trance that was very different from the one at work. That was prosaic – this was soothing. He liked to look down and feel the breeze on his face.

Five stories is a long way to fall. From five stories up you have to pass five windows, five lives. In one you might see a naked man drunkenly masturbating. In the second, an argument that's been brewing for weeks. The third – empty. This goes on until your eyes meet those at ground level that look out at the water colour sky a fraction of a second before you hit the warm pavement, not with a bang but with a surprisingly quiet thud. And you know that those eyes will look at the sky differently for a long time to come.

Like all the great tales, and even some of the mediocre ones, falling five stories would have a beginning, a middle and an end. Everything does.

If each leaping suicide had a story for every storey they sailed on by, Sam thought, then they could write them down and have a unique anthology of pre-death portraits. Travel always brings out the best in people.

With the whispering wind turning into a low-pitched whistle and time stretched out like a tangle of shiny escalators, falling five stories would be like an endless night time lullaby that lowers you into sleep. Five stories, one for each school night.

Falling five stories in secluded spots would be self-defeating, pointless. Or maybe the pointlessness *is* the point, thought Sam. No, that would be like visiting a gallery of blank canvasses, where even the curator sits sleepily daydreaming of some drying paint to observe. Five stories of free-falling though and suddenly you're the masterpiece, twitching to be framed or bound in print and placed in a library where shelves are never needed and membership is free to everyone.

Sam thought about these things and he looked at the gallery of frozen souls. He thought about these things when he fucked her as she dug her nails into his back. He thought about these when he woke up, He flicked through magazines and he saw photos on every page, smiling or scowling back at him. When he wasn't at work he was stoned and contemplating the portraits. When he thought about the portraits he usually felt pretty good, like it was his private thing.

Starved of conversation in the back room of the chemist, Sam started talking to the girls when he arrived back home. He had a full days worth of things to tell them. He shared his dreams and ambitions. He asked them questions and opinions and replied on their behalf. He lay on his back, a cushion behind his head, a large spliff hanging from his mouth and listened to the couple downstairs argue whilst he stared at the gallery knowing that he was stronger and better than everyone else. He never thought about work. He just went there and things happened and when he went home to his two dimensional harem. He wanked over some of them, confided in others and began to stop returning the girls' calls.

He never went out, apart from to the shops for cigarettes or to work, but even then he was inside. Inside, where he couldn't breath. Only now, his chest rarely tightened and his cigarette breaks became more leisurely. He walked more casually and never hurried himself over anything. Each day he slowly fed films into the machine and collated the results and each day a new face joined his gallery. He felt more ease and considered asking the owner to replace the air conditioning. Just an idea.

The nights began to get lighter – not that Sam ever really noticed, but it was nice to know that the seasons never let you down. It was nice to know that summer was still coming.

It was nice to know that nothing ever really changed, only those around you.

The gallery spread. Sam now had rows and rows of photographs, each depicting a completely unique female. Women all of ages looked down upon him from the off-white wall now. They laughed, they cried, they sulked and shouted - they were a rowdy bunch. The gallery covered half of the wall and, if you craned your neck and knew where to look, you could see it from way down on the street, the gloss surface reflecting the soft light of Sam's one-bedroom flat.

The evenings became hotter and Sam drank his wages and watched some TV, but mostly he conversed with the gallery. He began to think new thoughts, see the bigger picture. It excited him. A hundred women adorned the wall and Sam considered taking them all on holiday with him. Somewhere warm and light and with clean white walls. Somewhere to breathe. Somewhere like Spain. From now on, Sam decided, he was only going to live in the future.

joan jobe smith
Long Beach, USA

Shane, Coming Back

My father ruined the movie 'Shane' for me
in 1953 the last time he, my mother and I'd
go to a drive-in movie together before
movies became boring or biblical, me
in the back seat listening to him mock
Brandon De Wilde all through the movie:
"Shane, what you doin that for?" "Shane,
Shane, " my father would mock because he
hated that little kid, a tow-head brat he
called him. Why isn't that kid doing any
chores? That's what little boys do on the
farm, they don't go around asking a bunch
of fool questions and for all these years
I've never been able to watch that movie
without hearing my father's complaints
until last night when it finally dawned
on me: my father saw himself as that
little boy, a tow-head too a picture of
him at age 8 on our bedroom wall my father
squinting into the Texas sun holding his
gun he shot jackrabbit or squirrel for supper
that old picture taken just before his
mother came home from prison, gone two
years for forging her rich brother's name
on a $10 check, the brother that old mean
bastard turning her in to the sheriff my
father turned over to his grandfather
another mean bastard who put him to work
my father's own father, no Van Heflin, long gone.
"Shane, Shane come back Shane" my father
mocked once a day all this life after
seeing that movie, last night that last
scene even bringing tears to the eyes of
my big, strong machinist husband.

Have I Told You Lately That I Love You?

After reading John Bayley's eulogy book
about his beloved genius wife Iris Murdoch
and after drinking too much bourbon again
I get lugubrious and whiny (as usual)
and ask Fred why doesn't he write
about me, my belovedness (if I
have any), my genius (hah!), write
poems about my good cooking (true, so
Fred thinks), my virtue (maybe true),
my beauty (used-to-be maybe true) and Fred says

I will, I will, I'll write poems about you.
Someday. When you're dead.

But I want to read poems about me now, I whine.
While I'm alive.

So he writes a poem about me: about me
drinking too much bourbon and getting
lugubrious and whining to him to write me
poems about me: my tall, dark, handsome
poet husband making all my dreams come true.

When Gentlemen Preferred Go-Go Girls

We were shameless Mitzi and me
in 1973 bra-less in our tight
tank tops and bellbottom jeans
our hair swinging above our hips
lunching at the airport sipping
margaritas in the bar waiting
for our table the businessmen
with briefcases en route to
commute Frisco, Vegas giving us
the evil eye thinking us hookers
instead of the retired go-go girls
we were: me going to college for
the knowledge her getting into
gardening. What joy sitting
in that bar looking out at the
tarmac out the window where we'd
wave at Mitzi's lover she'd had
eight years because she refused
to leave her husband (because of
the kids). Isn't Kenny cute she'd
say and lust for his biceps as he
waved back on his way to the hangars
to clear off his desk where they'd
have good sex behind a locked door
after she and I had dessert and
we didn't say one word of this
yesterday when we talked on the
phone our yearly get-together as
we share our latest news of grandchildren
aches and pains cortisone injections
hers in the shoulders mine in the toe.
She golfs now, still gardens, her
husband helping her now and I still
write poetry but married now to a
good man and even though Mitzi and me

are still pretty much the same
only our bodies changing not our souls
we're sadly not shameless anymore
saying goodbye, dear, like sweet old
ladies, neither of us mentioning although
it must've been on her mind it sure
was mine: how she and Kenny used to
ride on his motorcycle in the middle
of the night after our go-go girl
nightshift all the way to Laguna Beach
to make love in the sand and fog
the two of them so turned on by
the bike's good, good, good, good
vibrations and excitations they
didn't even kiss first.

Lucky I Wasn't Wild Wendy or Dingy Dina

For years I've kept the love notes
all those years I go-go'd men wrote me
on the backs of peeled and dried Bud and
Coors bottle labels those in-coming
and out-going Vietnam marines asking
for first or last dates, notes on backs
of business cards from aerospace execs
(who'd been downsized), real estate
brokers (who'd soon get rich quick),
bankers, professors, bakers, candlestick
makers, beggarmen and thieves saying
"Call me any old time" even one time
from an archaeologist I said yes to for
dinner who showed me his trunks full
of gold he'd mined in South America and
smuggled to California and gave me two
1000-year old stone beads and a head, a
phallic symbol he said, embarrassing to
hold in my hand but when he showed me the
photo of him standing outside a grass hut
next to his Brazilian Indian wife and children
I said I had a headache and left him holding
our reservations to the swankiest place in
L.A. and boy was he lucky I wasn't Wild Wendy
or Dingy Dina with the bad-ass boyfriends
who would've come back and burgled him.

And today I've dumped my big box of old
love notes onto the kitchen table to
stir through them again, re-read them
memory lane all stained with beer,
scarred with cigarette ash burns, musty
with three decades of dust inside my
rolltop desk where I've kept them
those once-applications for the Job of Love,

Badges of my Red Courage when I shook my
tail feathers and let it all hang out 7 years.
I search with the earnest of a personnel
director and the FBI for the Right One
My Prince amongst the Frogs knowing that
if I'd interviewed them face-to-face for
20 years I'd never have found him.

Woodchuck

When his alarm clock goes off at 4 a.m.
I'm as awake as he is, feeling taut
and ready for action as the first
thing I remember is what he said
last night about his fellow worker
throwing a 100-pound Hartford chuck
across the shop floor, angry, mourning
that the place is closing down after
68 years in business, another big fish
corporate takeover. Later I'd call
the chuck a woodchuck by mistake
making my husband laugh and kiss my
foolish malaprop cheek (you know how
women don't know these things like
he doesn't know basil from tarragon).

And all night while I tried to sleep
I saw that man throw the chuck over
and over again across the concrete
floor where tin walls have contained
him for 20 years, where, in only months
will stand condos after the corporation
sells the land where men since 1932
thousands of men maybe a million
had jobs making airplanes for the
airlines and then the wars and then
the jets and spacecraft, jobs in the
office, jobs in the tool cribs, jobs
in the aisles and upon the concrete
and asphalt floor tile, only 40 jobs
left yesterday as the man threw the
chuck and screamed a profanity as furry
creatures ran and hid behind the trees.

The Star of David

My husband worries about the Star of David
hanging in the window, the first thing
anyone sees when they walk into our
apartment, worries the wrong people
will think we're Jewish and I once
thought I was on my Jobe side till
cousin James searched genealogy and
discovered we were from Wales and so
relieved was he he had tattooed on his
arm the Welsh flag but I still may be
Jewish on my mother's side and besides
I like to cover all my bases religionwise
and on my wall hangs the Madonna's head
from Michelangelo's "Pieta," draped
across a lamp is my tarnished silver
and mother-of-pearl crucifix, my
conversion gift from my old beau Joe.
Next to my bed sits an alabaster Buddha
and a plastic one sits on my rolltop desk
to whom I often offer grapes, chocolate
and prayer. And the Baha'i pamphlets
Touba gave me sit on the bookshelf
alongside the King James edition of
the Bible which contains my 4th grade
perfect attendance certificate to Baptist
Sunday school and proof of my 1948 baptism
which sits next to Baruch's "Why I Am
Not a Christian" and Whitman's "Leaves
of Grass," a Jehovah Witness "Watchtower,"
Bukowski's "Crucifix in a Deathhand,"
a trilobyte and my astrology chart that
reveals I was a woman in my last life
and will die an honorable death in this one.
But still my husband worries about the
Star of David because of the skinheads

and neo Nazis and the new women's Ku Klux
Klan movement who expound their "racist
consciousness" as proudly as if they've
made lead into gold these many mini
holocausts surrounding us zig-zag
crosshatch all over the face of
the globe but I want to keep my Star of
David, a little blue and green leaded glass
art project my daughter made in 6th grade
for her Jewish friend Debbie I wouldn't
let her give away because it was so beautiful.

By the Light of the Silvery Moon

A lot of learning doth make thee mad
Said my reborn Christian mother the
Decade I went to college for the knowledge.
Ignorance is bliss she said and meant it
And when I was writing my thesis the
Typewriter clacking all day driving her
Crazy as she lay ill down the hallway
In her white bedroom she called it my
Feces not out of disrespect but because
She was from Texas and that's how it
Sounded to her. I tried to tell her
That I was trying to make something
Of myself but she'd say she never read
Anything in a book she ever wanted to know
And where there's a will there's a way.

She only went to fourth grade in the
Dust Bowl Texas dry summer icy winter
Plains because she didn't have any shoes
And the other kids made fun of her and
Her daddy that old ignorant cowpoke didn't
Want her to go anyway and made pot shots
With his pistol when the truant officer
Came round to fetch her and her brothers
And sisters. They were needed at home
To help cook and care for the babies and
Pick cotton for the landlord and it was
This work ethic that my mother believed
In, a sweating brow, stretching muscles
Smooth fluid body and soul cleaniless next
To godliness and after I finished my thesis
And never got that respectable teaching post,
I used my thick bound thesis for a
Doorstop the malaprop feces not far off from
Its true definition and value to my being.

Maureen O'Hara

My father and I mourned when my mother cut her
hair chocolate-colored curly she wore during
World War Two halfway to her waist all that hair
she rolled into cake and pinned with Billy Holiday
gardenias, hair she white-turbaned Lana Turner
hair she upswept flower petal Maureen O'Hara
hairnetted Rosie the Riveter, plaited Jeanne
Craine braids on a beach picnic farmgirl in jeans
and a peasant blouse, how my father and I mourned
in 1951 when she chopped it off at her jaws
old Joan Crawford and in 1955 whacked it pixie
Leslie Caron cute. But my father said she looked
like a boy and we sadly knew she'd never let it
grow again and she never did. Marriages never end
because of hair but I was certain that it did when
my father left in 1957 when my mother looked like
Barbara Stanwyck: if only you'd let it grow
I thought age 17 and he'd come back even though
mine was duck-tailed and spit-curled like Kim Novak's
and even when he did come home she still trimmed it
short, short during the Doris Day bubble, short
instead of Dear Abby flip when my father died in
1966. Short when the hippies wore hair for shawls
short during disco blow-fluff. Please let it grow
I asked her as she lay dying in 1986, her hair
a thick chocolate-marshmallow crown. She wouldn't.
She demanded her granddaughter to chop it chemo
short and all I really wanted from my mother
for 35 years was one lock of her hair. Just one.

roddy lumsden
London, England

Lumsden Hotel

The kilted porter shook my hand in welcome,
drained it of blood and gave me back my luggage.
I signed the register in my own name
for the first time in a half-life of celebrity.
In the lounge bar, there were pictures by Margarita
but no sign of margaritas by the pitcher.
All night, the couple in the next room
failed to make love even once.
The song of the air conditioning
was a surefire B-side for any top one hundred hit.
I ordered up the late night menu
from room service, but sleep wasn't on it
so, after an hour of mentally undressing myself,
I donned the pyjamas with the killer bee motif
and sat on the bed and wrote a dozen
identical postcards to friends I'd forgotten.
No doubt to keep the cold tap company,
the hot tap had decided to be a cold tap too.
Funnel-web spiders wove their lazy way
toward each other across the ceiling
and when I turned on the shower,
there was no blood, but no water either.
By the bed, a Gideon Bible in Esperanto
and a phone-book listing Lumsdens of the world;
in the mini-bar, flat Vimto and a half-pint
of someone else's mother's milk, turned to fur.
The TV had only one channel, showing highlights
of my worst performances in every sphere.
At three, in the courtyard, a chambermaid choir
sang a barbershop version of 'I Will Survive'.
The only time I dared close my eyes,
the dervishes under the bed began to talk dirty.
When I left at nine and settled my check,
they told me clearly *Don't come back.*

My Water

The ox-bow lake where every creature
is the final generation of its species.
The river bottom where the proving's done.
The dish-slops where the mince-grease sails,
blown by the whore's-blench of my breath.
The wishing well run dry. A mill wheel
rusted to whimsy. Prisms in the sluice.
The bath gone cold before you're into it.
There's aye some water whaur the stirkie drouns.
Atlantic and Pacific. Streams of piss.
The days I wasted by the Maiden Rock
building dams where cold, cold water
tripped down from the farmer's fields,
to stop my life becoming all it is.

Reconstruction

When they asked me to name a *real* man,
it was you I thought of -
stamping on your parched floor,
speaking half a dozen instruments,
playing in a dozen languages,
unbuttoning the darkness to reveal
the pure, clear lie -
though now I think again, I don't know why.

My First Crush
(from *Roddy Lumsden is Dead*)

Everything can be neatly explained away by
something in our childhoods, so they say,

like Church St down to King's X, one Saturday a
month or so ago, when one young lady

sat opposite me, swung up on the galley
seats - the spit of Milly Molly Mandy -

and bit her fingernails the whole long way.
That's it. That's all I feel a need to say.

fred voss
Long Beach, USA

The Voice Of The Woman Who Needs You

Stay still for one hour
and all the stars will begin to move around you
stay still for one hour
and every glass on every table
and each rushing of a car down a street
will tell how lost we are stay still
and you will have a chance
to find your way stay still
and you may finally hear
the song of the bird on the wire high above the alley
and what your father
tried to tell you when you were 6 the fog
dripping off a steel railing on your balcony the heart
breaking in the voice of the woman who needs you stay still
and you may be ahead of the millions hurtling down freeways
at 70 mph you may see
for the first time the 100-year-old ironwork
on a 3rd-story window or the language
in the fingers of the steelcutter as he moves them sitting on a stool
    looking off
at the far corner of a factory ceiling stay still
and the ant crawling across the sidewalk
will be enough
as all the knots that you have never been able to untie loosen
just a little
and all the dragonflies set off on flights
and there is no limit
to what you may do this Sunday morning
at 5:57 am.

Learning To Love Earplugs

The 30-foot-long 20-foot-tall Verson
hydraulic press across the aisle from my machine
had always made so much growling grinding slamming noise
that I had had to stuff earplugs into my ears
under the headphones I was already wearing,
so I was glad
when it finally broke down.
6 men from Maintenance
in white overalls with red tags on their pockets
were climbing up and down and all over and around
the Verson,
tossing wrenches and channel-lock pliers back and forth
and shouting
out their observations and opinions about how to fix
it as they cranked up
the 6,000-tons-of-hydraulic-pressure metal-bending machine
and SLAMMED it through its paces 3 times louder than it had ever slammed
before
until
suddenly a huge geyser of hot stinking milky hydraulic oil
shot up 40 feet in the air out of a hole
in the center of the top of the machine
and drenched the ceiling beams and floodlights and rained down
in a fine mist
all over my head and lunchpail and newspaper and work   bench
and I heard
from one of the machinists quickly gathered in a circle about the disaster
how on the weekend just a few days before
Maintenance had almost blown
the Verson's bladder and sent 750 gallons of stinking oil
raining down all over the entire building and caused the side lid
to the Verson's huge barrel to shoot off
and kill anyone who might have been standing in its path.

Suddenly having to stuff earplugs into my ears didn't seem so bad.

Nuts And Bolts And Men

Asked by one machinist his opinion of another machinist
a machinist may slam down his wrench and say,
"What a worthless piece of shit! That son of a bitch is the most
USELESS son of a bitch I've ever seen!"
loud enough for his opinion to he heard
in a 5 machine radius.
A 5-foot-2-inch machinist
may stand like he's 6-foot-5
and shout out so loud his words echo off the tin walls,
"He's the biggest ASSHOLE west of the Mississippi!!"
Machinists may wrinkle their noses up into their heads
like they are smelling dogshit
or spit onto the concrete floor
and twist their mouths like they are about to puke.
"That motherfucker can suck my dick!!"
"FUCK him! That arrogant lazy bad breath son of a bitch takes it up
the ass without any Vaseline!"
they may shout
without bothering to look around once to see if the man
they are
speaking about
is within earshot.

Everywhere you look in a machine shop there are nuts and bolts and men
saying exactly what they think.

One Button Off A Dead Son's Shirt

Will a man on his deathbed really care
that computers have covered the globe
with their net?
Will he really care
if the phone beside him can reach anywhere on earth
or a plane
down the street at the airport take him
anywhere or encyclopedias
of information be available at the click
of his computer mouse?
Will it really seem important to him that c.d. players
can pick out any exact second in a symphony by Beethoven
and begin playing there
or that 15 sports events are available to him at the same time
on television?
Will it comfort him
that we have flattened the earth into submission
with condos and mansions and parking structures and double-decker freeways
and any given minute buy and sell more
than he can ever conceive of?
Or would he not rather have one button
off a dead son's shirt,
be
one fraction of an inch closer
to understanding what Beethoven meant,
know
there may be something in him that will burn with the last star until it has
    exploded
into cinder,
touch
the hand of his poor wife who has nothing
but him?

Too Big For Tin Walls To Hold

Machinists don't just urinate
they swagger up to sheet metal machine shop bathroom troughs
and say, "Is this where the BIG DICKS hang out?"
and pull out their cocks
and piss
3-foot-long arcs into the troughs
so that their piss is hammering against the sheet metal
as they smile.
Machinists don't just get a tattoo
they cover their bodies
with large red and green and black and blue
tattoos of black widows
and cobras and skulls smoking cigarettes and dominatrixes
with long whips.
They don't just curse supervisors under their breath
but shout out nicknames for them like "MussoWEENIE!"
and hang wire and shop rag tails
from their rear belt loops
and orchestrate dedicated and relentless campaigns
to try to give them heart attacks.
They don't just walk across a machine shop floor
but part
the air with each swing of their hand
and stride of their leg
and turn and cock of their head
like
the greatest painter or poet on earth
could never be luckier
than if he captured them
for eternity.

Cadillacs

I am so glad to be one
of these machinists and painters and tube benders and polishers and craters
and packers
as we flood across the black asphalt on our way home
Friday
and the upper manager parts us with his Cadillac
driving through.
I am so glad to be one
of these men who don't know if they'll have a job next week
rather than in
that car and the suit of that man who studies
and judges and condemns us to our fates with a sweep of his hand
across layoff notices.
I am so glad to be one
of the ones in cheap tank tops with bare arms and shoulders who don't know
where they will be
next week,
who never have to study
or judge or condemn one man
as they cut steel into parts they can hold in their hands
and earn their dollars
by the sweat on their backs,
I am so glad I never used my college degree to become
the man
in that suit
in the shadows inside that car
but am one of these men flooding out the gate
toward a sun
that still feels as good on our bare skin as it did
when we were 5 years old.

Clearing The Air

After the quitting buzzer blares
and we machinists have punched out and are striding
across asphalt to the gates Max
turns around and grins and shouts,
"Hi Shorty!"
to 5-foot 2-inch Paul who
raises himself up on the balls of his feet and sticks his jaw out and lifts
his chin and shouts back,
"Hey Baldy! I guess you lost all your brains along with your hair huh Baldy!"
and immediately
all the bald men and the short men
among us are screaming insults at each other
until the bunch of us explodes
into screamed top-of-our-lungs insults
about each other stinking
or being fat
or having bad breath or ugly faces
or little dicks
or beards that look like cunt hair
as we stick our middle fingers
up out of our fists and wave and corkscrew them around
over our heads flipping each other
the bird
before we get into our cars to race away from each other.

Not having to see each other's faces for another 16 whole hours
calls for a little
celebration.

He Won't Be On News At 5

In the computer lab
of the Career Transition Center where we ex-Goodstone Aircraft Company
workers go to look for jobs
as Goodstone closes down our plant
the ex-aircraft skin riveter
can't stop talking.
"They talk about all the jobs out there! What they don't talk about is how all
those jobs are jobs that pay $6 or $7 an hour! Or they're part time so you're
only working 30 or 35 hours a week and they don't have to give you benefits!
Yeah, there's lots of jobs but they're jobs you can't live on!"
he shouts
in the tiny low-ceilinged room
in his cowboy hat he always wears because he always wore it
while he was riveting aircraft skins.
"Yeah now my car's broke down! Now I'm ridin' buses! I need $1100 to get the
transmission fixed! And I'm supposed to take a job for $6 an hour!"
he goes on shouting, unable to stop
as all the men with their faces in front of computers looking for work try
to ignore him.
"Yeah they talk about the low unemployment rate! But they don't talk about
how after you use up your 6 months unemployment they don't count you as
unemployed anymore! You just drop out of sight and you're no longer one of
the unemployed! It's all politics! It's all stinkin' POLITICS! They already
know who's president. BIG MONEY'S PICKED HIM!"

He just can't stop shouting at the walls
in his neat impeccable white shirt and cowboy hat
like he's surprised.

The last thing he'd expected to have this morning was
a nervous breakdown.

Just What They Wanted To Hear

At the Goodstone Aircraft Company Career Transition Center
45
and 55-year-old men and women were gathered
at tables up and down the huge union hall to hear
the financial advisor
from the finance firm talk to them
about their financial future
now that they were being laid off from their $22-an-hour jobs.
Aging
hippies with beard braids down to their waists
and tired
middle-aged women who had done nothing but rivet aircraft skins all their lives
and terrified Indians and blacks old before their time but still
too young to retire trembled inside
and listened
to the young sharp-as-a-tack-in-his-$1,000-suit
executive
glib with all the money he'd made
for the rich in the stock market
scold them
about investing their money wisely and building up a nest egg.
"You'd better do it now before you end up 70 years old and having to work as
a greeter at K-Mart!"
he yelled
at them with all of his 25-year-old M.B.A.
brilliance and assurance
as the fact
that they very well might end up having to take
$6-an-hour jobs
stared them in the face
and they looked at that young man in his shiny suit like he might as well
have been
from another planet.

Going To His Corner

Gus
smiles his sweet
butter-wouldn't-melt-in-his-mouth wouldn't-hurt-a-fly
smile
all day every day as he walks
with shoulders hunched on little cat's feet
about our machine shop visiting one machinist
after another for months
not raising his voice one bit or casting one mean glance
until
over in a corner by himself
one morning he suddenly explodes hurling
bolts against a wall snapping them
in 2 and screaming
in rage as he breaks
cutters and tools hurling them down
into the concrete floor that explodes
as he gouges it
apart ranting and raving
and kicking cabinets and machines
for no reason anyone is aware of
and no one ever finds out about.
Then
he immediately goes back to his angelic smiling
and walking-on-eggshells
wouldn't-harm-a-fly
visiting-everyone-in-the-shop friendliness
for months.

A man has to resort to something
when he can't afford psychotherapy.

peter didsbury
Hull, England

PETER DIDSBURY INTERVIEWED

This interview with Jules Smith took place at the author's house in Hull, on 24 March 2000.

JS I'd like to start, Peter, by asking you about your early experience of readings. What were the readings at the outset of your career like, especially those done with your then-young friends?

PD We had this poetry show at the beginning of the 1980s called 'Verbals', for want of a better phrase a multi-media show. It was a vehicle for half a dozen people - myself, Douglas Houston, Sean O'Brien, and others - to read poems, before our first books had come out. It was also for whatever line up of rock band that Sean was drumming in at the time, and for some talented local comedians. We only did this show 4 or 5 times. We took it on the road to Lincoln on one occasion, two or three times at the Spring Street theatre. Basically we each had a slot and read about seven poems. After one peformance, a member of the audience came up and said that we had all stood there smoking and saying that the next poem would be 'self-explanatory'.

JS What interests me about that is from the way you describe it, it seems theatrical, with stage elements and music. Which is at odds with the kind of reading you now do. Is it the case that you learned at that period that the theatrical and extrovert reading was not for you?

PD I don't think there's that kind of contrast. I mean, we were standing up and reading some serious poems. It's just that they were set in this vehicle of comedy and music. There were more 'experimental' things...such as Doug Houston shovelling gravel on stage, while I wrote Persian calligraphy in emulsion paint on a big screen. [laughs] At first, I was very loathe to read at all, for nervous reasons. For the first Verbals show I in fact recorded my poems. They were played in a darkened theatre. I was as 'Radio Darkness'. [laughter] A single spotlight lit up my old twin tub washing machine. The show's comedian walked out onto the stage and ritually opened one of the lids of the twin tub, and then my poems came out of there. [more laughter] Having done that, I thought I can't let all these guys do it and not do it myself. So I read one poem in person, and liked it so much that it broke my fear of public readings.

JS Right. But who were the poets you first saw reading live, and did you think you could learn from them?

PD I probably hadn't seen many poets at all until I was well into my thirties. I would have seen Douglas [Dunn]. For me there was probably no pattern as to how to read. I still don't go to many readings. In periods like the *Bete Noire* years [in Hull 1985-94] I was a fairly regular attender. I mean, most poets don't try to be BBC actors - the worst people to read poems - but they try to put whatever emotion is necessary into it. The odd person like Paul Durcan stands out; a magic reader, a magician. No, you just get up and do it and hope you get better really.

JS Yes. The single *Bete Noire* reading which stands out in my mind was that one you did with Paul Durcan. [10 February 1988] Apart from the emotion of the evening there was a great contrast, between your undemonstrative manner and the bardic style of Durcan. I remember that John Osborne [editor-impresario of *Bete Noire*] also put you on with Robert Creeley and Carol Ann Duffy.

PD Yes, I enjoyed reading with Carol Ann, and Bob Creeley on two occasions. Memorable times, and superb get-togethers afterwards.

JS Have you ever sat there at a reading and thought that you should be doing more to 'sell' your work, in the way they do?

PD No, though I think I am fairly extrovert with the audience now. I certainly feel very much like an actor when I'm doing it, and can understand what actors say about how you can judge what's happening out there in the darkness. During the Andrew Motion reading [at the Hull Truck theatre in November 1999, also with Tony Griffin] the audience was palpably a presence. I've done a fair few readings, but I'm not really on the circuit, at a different place each week. I remember that the experience of sitting behind Durcan was quite startling. He starts off in a low voice, which compels the audience to prick up their ears...[laughs] I do enjoy reading to an audience, and what I also get out of it is more or less re-creating the experience of writing the poem, when you're declaiming it. 'Declaiming' is a good word, I think, because there is a rhetorical element to my poetry. And to re-create the rhetoric that went into the making of it is a real high. You always know if it's working because there's this wave of feedback from the audience.

JS It seems to me, having been to a number of your readings over the years, that the way you read is perfectly complimentary to your subject matter. In the sense that your exotic imagination, the language used which is sometime recondite and literary...if you had a theatrical performance of that, it would be too much really. It constantly surprises me the way that audiences have a rapport with your work, the way they latch onto it. You've got certain exotic scenarios in your poems, sometimes complex and even theological material, yet they appreciate them. Is this to do with storytelling, as your longer poems do tell stories?

PD I don't read any of the longer poems very often; I read my middle-length and shorter ones. I would love to read the longest poem I've written, 'The Devil On Holiday', but it takes 13 minutes. I'm not sure that's the kind of thing you inflict on an audience. I follow some basic rules about planning the reading: alternate the short and longer poems, the lyric with something else, have a funny one in every third poem. It sounds crude, but they are there for an evening out. You can prime them with a certain amount of stuff that goes between the poems, so they'll get that percentage out of the poem as it's being read.

JS I'd still say that it surprises me the way that audiences catch on to the fantastic elements in your work. For instance, 'That Old-Time Religion', which is a complex piece alluding to Sumerian poetry, 'Paradise Lost', and a poem by the Victorian poet Arthur Hugh Clough. It has a storyline in which God and the angels are decked out as 1930s aristocrats, and records the repartee between them. Every time I hear you read it, the audience does get the complex joking that is going on. The line which always gets a laugh is when chainsmoking God has a logical error pointed out to him by the Devil, and flicks the ash from the end of his cigarette, "displeased at His foreknowledge of where it will fall".

PD Yeah, I know. It's the one line that never fails. [laughs] In a sense, when they laugh I get a re-creation of the pleasure I got when I wrote it. You say that the poem is dealing with difficult matters of textuality. But there's a false antithesis here. How it got written was that I sat down at the kitchen table bored one evening with a beer...

JS You weren't influenced by Charles Bukowski, were you? [laughter]

PD No comment! This idea comes into your mind - you suddenly see God and the angels in dinner suits on the terrace in a Noel Coward play. It just flows from there, because of where I live now, the society I live in. The audience lives in the same world. That's how they can understand it. Poetry has to be about finding some common ground. Maybe readings are where people realise occasionally that poetry is for them.

JS If this was a radio interview, the DJ would now ask some thing like "What was the worst reading you've ever done?" [laughs]

PD The worst I can remember was at Huddersfield. I went along on a Sunday lunchtime with Pat, Sarah [their daughter] and George Messo. The pub was a converted Victorian Bank, with a glass dome; the Spring sun came in and it was atrociously hot. The Espresso coffee machine on the bar kept hissing, and the doors were open to the next bar. You couldn't hear yourself think, let alone read. Another famously awful one was during a series of lunchtime readings at Spring Street theatre in about 1981 or 82. Our audience of seven faithfuls was there, including three old ladies. In the middle of this particular reading I was doing, some workmen came in and started moving a piano. It was Doug Houston who muttered darkly about "piano-shifting brutalists". [laughter]

JS Your work has a lot of playfulness and humour.

PD Some of it does. It is a grim humour sometimes. [sighs]

JS People who don't share your interests are nevertheless able to understand and enjoy your work...

PD Obviously today there's no common ground that eveyone assents to in anything. But we live in the same world. You don't have to understand Einstein yet everyone lives Relativity. It's a question of finding a balance. When you start off writing, you fall constantly into the error of being too particular and personal. You've got to be true to a very personal idiom and remain this side of accessibility. The more you are true to the eccentricity of yourself the more you will find people understanding it. It's a conversation I've had with many poets. The deeper you can go into your specifics, the more likely you are to find an audience.

JS Can I change tack and ask you about your job and how it relates to your poetry over the years? It's always struck me that your employment as an archaeologist suggests ways in which to read it. For instance, in terms of layering, and with past culture in bits. Would you say that it has suggested subject matter to you?

PD A lot of my poetry was written before I became established as a professional archaeologist, though I've always been interested. Archaeology isn't a romantic thing to do, as it's practised today. It's very data-oriented. You're looking at patterns of past rubbish disposal. It is structured towards satisfying developer funding, which is liable to empty any notions of romance rather than encourage poetry.

JS So you wouldn't say that your job has had...if not a direct influence, then a kind of general analogy in your work? In your third book, *That Old-Time Religion*, there are some poems which seem related, pre-historical scenes suggested by your job, if only as a dream. I'm thinking of a poem like 'At Her Grinding Stone'.

PD I do think "At Her Grinding Stone' is an archaeological poem, with a definite link to what I was doing at the time. I was excavating a wetlands site between Cottingham and Hull, an Iron Age/Romano-British site. One of the finds was a quern [grinding stone] which had been thrown into a spring on the margins of a settlement. I'd been working outside every day in the Autumn. It was a sort of reverie about life in those Iron Age roundhouses. But what is interesting about the poem is that it's the only one in which I've inhabited a female personality, the only character a scornful woman. And what she's scornful about is...[sighs] the whole male set-up around her. I don't profess to understand why it happened, but it's a really important poem to me.

JS I can't think of any other poet who could write a poem like that. Do you feel part of contemporary poetry or slightly eccentric to it?

PD I suppose I would have to say eccentric to it still. Though less so than when I started out. I started publishing late. People called me a young poet until they could no longer get away with it. It's strange, the transition between the days when O'Brien, Griffin, Flynn and I were tyros, seizing any opportunity to meet, and drink, with the masters who were available in Hull...and suddenly you've got people coming up to you who've been reading your books. I did a reading a couple of years ago with a guy whose first book had just been published, and he said "It's been my ambition for years to read with you".

JS You do have that kind of status really, as a poet's poet.

PD I wish I were a book buyer's poet, you know. [laughs]

JS Writers who I meet from time to time, like Ian McMillan, Matthew Sweeney, and Jo Shapcott, really enthuse about your work. They know it well. And it's clearly not a case of them latching onto a particular fashionable author. It's just that they've found something unique. But it does seem to me that your work is very English and romantic, if in eccentric ways.

PD I think that when the first book came out, Peter Porter reviewed it in *The Observer* and used phrases like "seedy urban pastoral".

JS Just for my own interest, could you say something about the kind of stuff you were writing at Oxford and just after? You left Oxford in the late 1960s...

PD 1968. I actually started writing at school, Hymer's College. [Public School in Hull] There was a teacher in the Sixth Form, whose name needs recording: Mr 'Gary' Grayson. He was also a strong influence on Sean O'Brien, and Sean won't mind me saying that. Because poetry was his enthusiasm, he chose all the poetry options on the 'A' level syllabus, and he was telling us about William Empson, Gerard Manley Hopkins, John Donne *et al*. One week he didn't set an essay but asked us to these neologisms and sprung rhythms weren't some cavalier, 'let-it-all-hang-out' thing, but that it was disciplined, difficult and all the rest. After that, it was what I wanted to do.

JS From that time on, you wrote constantly?

PD I would have been 16, 17. Yes, I wrote continually from then on.

JS After you'd gone through the stage of writing pastiches, what were the first authentic poems like?

PD The first authentic ones...I'd been reading H.R. Ellis-Davidson on Norse myths in the Penguin edition. I wrote this poem with a line about "Odin hanging tree-bound, screaming to attain the runes". [laughs] It seems over the top, but it was directly out of my experience of reading. Looking back on the first dozen poems, which I've still got, there are about three that are original. Then for a while I was pastiching Eliot, writing all this dross about dry landscapes, old men and the dry vines. At University, I wasn't writing intelligent stuff at all. I was reading [Jacques] Prevert, for example.

JS You didn't meet any poets then who might have overlapped with your time at Oxford, people like James Fenton and John Fuller?

PD No, not at all.

JS I seem to recall some statement of Douglas Dunn's about "the often strange patterns of imagery and statement" that your work produces. [Introduction to *A Rumoured City*]. Fair comment, I think.

PD By the time Douglas first saw my work I was writing fairly accessibly, at least part of the time. A straightforward poem like 'Upstairs' in *The Butchers of Hull*, about swans on the drain, dates from that period. I still read it.

JS Did Douglas like your early work?

PD He did actually. Remarkably. He does have the characteristic of being generous about poetry he's not wholly in sympathy with. Before I knew him, he'd been encouraging people like Ian Gregson and Tony Griffin. I don't think Tony would mind being called 'surrealist' at that stage.

JS I'd like to know more about this period when your work developed rapidly. This was when you and Sean O'Brien were very competitive, both of you trying to impress Douglas Dunn and Norman Jackson?

PD I first met Sean in one of Norman Jackson's poetry workshops that he was running at Spring Street theatre, the year after I came back from Oxford. Sean was in his long vacation prior to going to Cambridge. We were doing this kind of writing for each other before any of us made Douglas's acquaintance. I still do find it strange, almost of cosmic significance [laughs] that Sean and I were at the same school. He claims to remember me giving him lines. [laughs] Then years later we bumped into each other. Then the fact that Doug Houston arrived back in Hull from Germany a couple of years later. That Douglas Dunn was available as a mentor. And that Larkin was always there in the background.

JS Sean was younger than you, and conspiciously ambitious. He was interested in poets like Auden and Peter Porter...

PD We shared a fairly eclectic common interest. The point is that we were both very ambitious, though we expressed it in different ways. We used to sit in the St. John's pub in the summer holidays, 'planning our assault on the citadel of English poetry'. He did say to me one evening that he wanted to be the best, his generation's Auden. The way history has turned out, I don't think there was the possibility for anyone to do that. Larkin was the last person who might have done it. We both thought that the best thing which could could happen to us - apart from getting laid that night [laughs] - was to get a 'slim volume' out.

JS This small band of writers have come to be known, in retrospect, as the Hull Poets, mainly due to the anthologies. Was it a male bonding thing? Were the women poets around Hull at the time, such as Genny Rahtz and Margot K. Juby, slightly marginalised by the competitive male atmosphere?

PD No, because there wasn't a deliberate policy. Genny is a great friend of mine and I have a marked respect for her poems. She had a young child at the time, and a different agenda. Apart from Margot, we simply didn't come across any other women poets. We met each other in pubs, swopped poems, enjoyed a lot of drinking, talking, smoking, and everything.

JS My peception is that the half dozen or so talents concerned developed quickly because of the intensity of all that. I'm struck every time I see some of you in the same room that you quickly go back into the same mode. I can mentally recapitulate the way in which you all used to interact.

PD It's great, yes. The funny thing is that Flynn and Griffin were a sub-fractional poetic generation. We weren't initially part of the same thing. They both started out as protegés of [Roy] McGregor-Hastie. [then a lecturer at Hull Training College; poet and translator of Rumanian poetry] Then they both left Hull. It was only after the launch of *A Rumoured City* [Bloodaxe, 1982] that we've become good friends. Tony Griffin comes to stay with us regularly. We weren't all together in the beginning.

JS So you really were a group like the Surrealists or the Objectives [laughs] in the sense that not all of you were ever in the same room at the time it was happening. It was much more loose...

PD It was loose and extended. It depends who you ask. If it is a cosmic accident, then it is an interesting one. To me it means a period of about three years in the early 1980s, marked by...everyone was going through personal crises, breaking up long-standing relationships. It meant that people were free to be out, talking about poetry, because there weren't any constraints upon them. Sean was back down here doing his Ph.D. I was divorced. People were in pubs five nights a week; there were musicians around like Johnny Solo, a lot of painters like Stuart Ross [who did the cover for *The Butchers of Hull*] and John Pettenuzzo. You knew that if you went to 'The Polar Bear' that someone would have a good poem. It spurred you on to be the one who had it next time.

JS Did you have anything to do with older writers like Frank Redpath, George Kendrick, and the looming figure of Philip Larkin?

PD Nobody ever saw Larkin, or hardly ever. People used to swop their 'Larkin Sightings'. It's quite amazing the number of people who will tell you Larkin stories and call him 'Philip'. I did meet him in 1982, when Sean, Douglas Dunn and I went to a reading at 'The Goodfellowship Inn'. Maybe Gavin Ewart was on. We'd thoroughly enjoyed the first half, but then saw Larkin in the bar during the interval and stayed downstairs. He turned out to be charming to talk to. I was then teaching his stuff on an 'A' level course, and heard myself asking him about the Irish sixpence [in 'Church Going']. He was quite willing to answer the question. But generally no, Larkin wasn't part of anything like that. In relation to Frank and George, they were people we'd known for years. Frank's problem was that he was always written off as the poor man's Larkin. In fact, they were of the same generation but...completely different politics. The formal similarities are superficial. He was writing in the modes available to him in the 1950s, as was Larkin.

JS I do think Frank was a decent writer, but he lacked the drive and ambition to 'get on' in the poetry world. They also differed totally in their taste in jazz, of course, Frank favouring bebop as opposed to Trad Jazz. Do you know the story I think Jean Hartley tells, that he wrote a message in the dust on Larkin's car? TREMBLE LARKIN - BIRD LIVES! [laughter]

PD George came along to those early Norman Jackson workshops. For me, *Bicycle Tyre In A Tall Tree* [Carcanet, 1974] was a wonderful collection. The title poem, though a lovely one, is a bit obvious. It becomes a bit of a cliché. But to paint Pearson Park in early Spring weather, with old men around the lake, and the lines "His chrome transistor jams/ the great inexpressible chords" [from 'Winter Sunshine'], that still seems to me to be something tremendous. And we shouldn't forget Norman; his ability to draw poetry out of people was amazing. He was billed as The Bricklayer Poet in the press, I recall, and then went on to the States with a place on the Iowa Creative Writing course. His poems were mainly short lyrics.

JS So this band of young writers did have living role models of more or less successful contemporary poets walking the streets of Hull. And there was this hot house poetry atmosphere. But what is the state of the game for you now? You've published three books since 1982. Have you enough poems in hand for a fourth?

PD No, nowhere near, but I'm working on it. I write more slowly now. It's due to the normal practical things of earning a living. But when I'm commissioned to do something, as Shane [Rhodes] did last year with the *Heartlands* anthology [Hull City Arts Unit, 1998], or the Salisbury Festival last year, it seems to bring you back into the orbit of being a poet. I wrote *The Classical Farm* in less than two years after the first book came out, but then it took Bloodaxe five years to put it out. One got a bit disillusioned.

JS When is your next reading?

PD Whenever someone asks me to do one. I'm available!

JS I remember that about five or six years ago *Marxism Today* carried an article on *Bete Noire*. In it, John Osborne was asked about the state of contemporary poetry and he encapsulated this by saying that you had stripped the wallpaper from a room, in your former house in Ventnor Street, and couldn't afford to decorate it.

PD It's the same in one room here now. [laughs]

JS You're still in more or less in the same position. Well-known to other poets, but your work is a niche market, even in poetry. Would you welcome more exposure?

PD What does one say to that? I do have an audience. I even get the occasional fan letter from New Zealand and other far away places. But I've never really wanted a reputation as one of the poetry world's movers and shakers. I would love to be in a situation again where I have more time to write poetry. I'm sure I'll always write. Poems surprise me even now.

JS If you were a celebrity poet, you might have all kinds of journalists camped out on your doorstep or searching for your ex-wives...

PD I've only got one. I must remind you that at a party you once said to Pat, "What's it like being married to a famous poet?" And do you remember what she replied? "He's just like any other husband. He doesn't do the washing up, and he farts in bed". [laughter] There's your answer.

Mediaeval, Somehow

I go to the second-hand bookshop,
to sell an unwanted saucepan.
Three young women sit bathing
in a high wooden tub in the window.
I wait while the man in front of me gets paid
in good English coin for a carrier full of skillets,
then it's the turn of myself and my singular pan.
Two quid. Five quid. Seven.
Timely acceptance serves to prevent
his offer from holing the roof,
but transactions like this
are never so easily ended.
Before I can leave I must taste the subtle pleasure
of watching my only just sold get purchased again.
Which might eventually happen,
'once mine' and 'never mine' together in the mouth
of a sack held open by a brown-robed mendicant,
smilingly there to refurbish a friary kitchen.

To Warm A House
For Martin and Gail

Bread. Salt. Wine. Verse. Song.

These gifts we bring,
Ungraced, I fear, by parcel-wrapper's art,
To wish you all
We hope you'll never lack.

Bring here this very night, that is,
To the newest abode
Of your lives' abiding,
Bread and salt,
The one home-baked
The other corner-shopped,
With the very best that Ernest and Julio
Have known how to tread,
Or Bloodaxe to anthologise.

And for song?
Well, Couperin,
To memorialise those lessons
That are only learned among shadows,
Respectfully asking
That they absent themselves tonight,
Unless gifted by guttering candles
To the tired but happy wreckage
Of an admired and fortunate feast.

And now, my friends,
Put back and leave these gifts in a carrier bag,
Deliberate to deflect the gaze
Of any wandering petty god
Who may hereabouts flit,
Susceptible to jealousy.
When you wake tomorrow, be reminded
That bread, salt, wine, verse, song

Each in its own way burns and hath sufficiency;
That hearth, heart, love and house,
Your lives and soon to be three lives life,
May all be lit and warmed thereby;
And that this, as now we seat ourselves at your table.
Is what we both, in unsolemn reverence, wish you.

Therefore Choose Life

It may have been the night I dreamed the machine code
that I took my latest step along the road
of realising just how strange
whatever it is that is going on here *is*.
I stood before the familiar inner screen,
the one that is both self and not-self,
and maybe also neither,
and watched as there slowly scrolled, unrolled,
an array of symbols principally composed
of bars and filled circles,
a kind of fat Morse, in all the primary colours.
And that's about it. In fact, its importance seems to reside
in the paucity of what there remains to say:
I was not amazed.
I don't remember any terminating transition.
That which I stood and watched did not require
me in any way to adopt a different posture.

The House Sitter's Letter
For Gentian

Thank you for lending us
your house and your cat
again this year.

We had no right to expect it.

She is called Pebble
and lives off dried food,
but of course you already know this.

And isn't it quiet here!
I feel I could borrow the name off your jar of pickles
and become a Chinese poet!

I would if it wasn't Woh Hup.

Woh Hup ...

Wasn't he the one
who dipped his drunken hair in ink
and filled a wall in the house of a friend
with swirling vermilion carp?

Actually
I'm much improved of late
and hardly batted an eyelid earlier on.
I don't say I approve
of cotton shirts behaving like that
in the humid midnight wind
but I'm assured I've come a long way.

Whereas *you*, of course,
have *gone* a long way. Away.
Away to your African drumming in Dumfries,
and look, I don't want you to

worry and spoil your retreat
but between you and me,
I think it's Pebble who's the nervous one.
You should see the way she behaves when it thunders,
you really should.

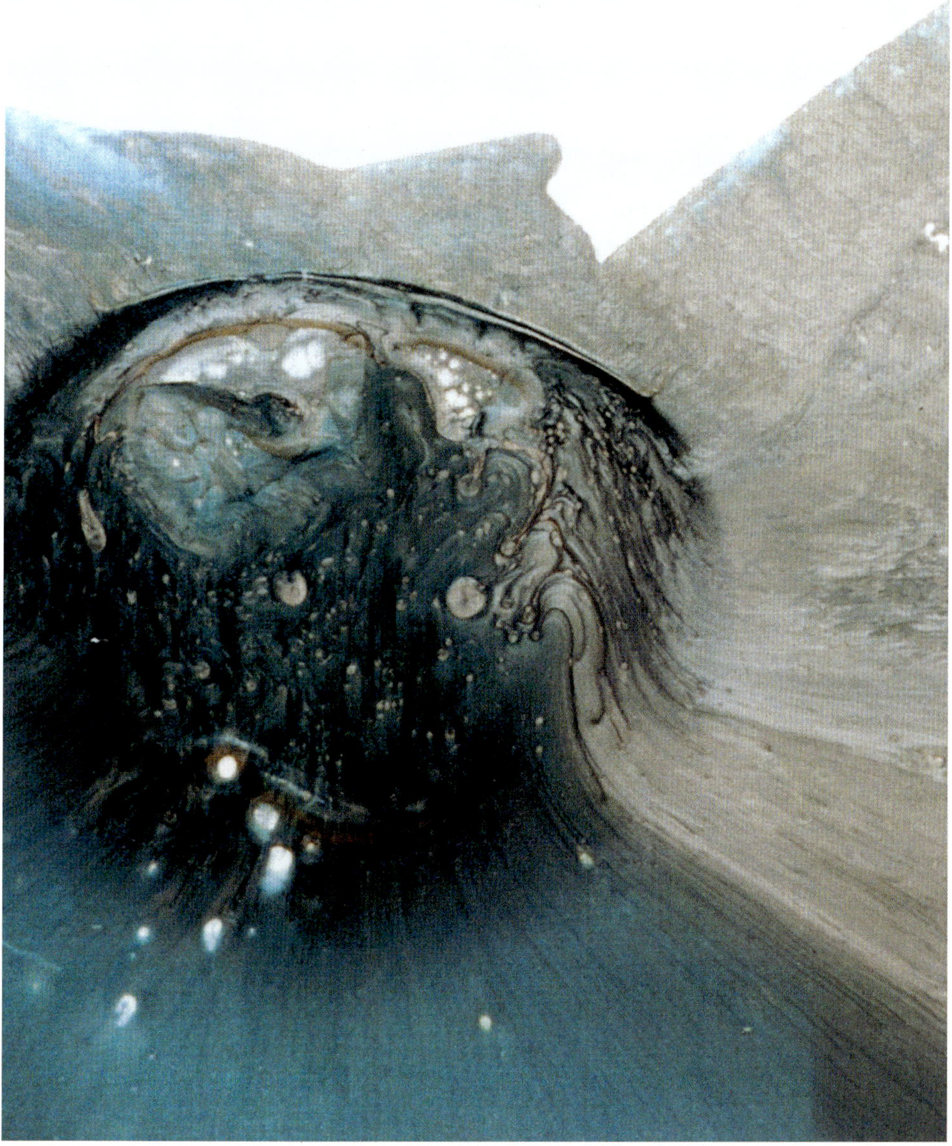

steve waling
Manchester, England

We Start With The Sea

                               then watch clouds
dragged rainfully off the horizon. We are not
in danger. It pours down because we're careless,
ploughs right through them. Those are the hills

and a coastline of beaches and ports with
painted white Monopoly houses. We don't
wave back to the ferry going the opposite way
but Phil says: *Look, the Wicklow Hills, I've*

been there before. A buoy gently bobbing
and Bob, a boy, pointing: Sue looks sceptical;
another sudden squall reads the waves, deep
as uncut books. Poor excuse for a storm but

we're hooked, reined in by the port. I gulp,
eyes swivel, two black holes on stalks.
We swim in perceptions as the sea sticks
a lighthouse finger up at visitors: *Welcome*

to Dublin. I bet it rains before land. It does: I win.
The prize: twin white chimneys ringed with red.
Wharves gleam like pictures of harbours in books
full of gantries, cranes, dockers oily with sweat

lifting and toting and creaming the top off.
We'll be in soon: nothing to declare but a hat
and questions. When did sailors stop singing
down gangplanks in films? A pilot boat wasps past,

makes its shrill announcement to the shore.

j. morris
Arlington, USA

Lines Written More In Anger Than In Sorrow

"Of course, as a chess player Bobby was a genius and as a political thinker he's a schmuck."
– An astute observer

Oh no, old green-eyes is back,
a shambling golem who knows two things:
Jew-hatred and chess.

Who let him in, who called him up
from the clay to play another day?
The Fischer-king

> has much to say about "Adolf's legacy,"
> sacred still, and "yet one more
> international Jewish conspiracy"
> that's turning Grandmasters into whores
>
> and barring godly men from dominance
> over the Russians – who hate the Jews
> as well, but are godless Communists –
> or were – and here it gets confused,
>
> but clarity isn't often enjoyed
> when you're paranoid.

Who indulged him, who took down his words,
who crowned him with authority?
He knows nothing

and is the most brilliant player
who ever lived. I'll concede
that chess takes talent,

if the concession helps me make
such a simple, simple point,
a point grasped by children

when they say of some bully,
*Oh, he's good at games but he's a
real dick,*

no one pays any attention to him,
but ignored by our drooling
media lords,

blinded by chess-smarts, eager
for hot quotes, ink-hounds hungry
for big bad bucks:

talent and virtue are unrelated.
Let Bobby have his brilliant mates
but go unquoted.
DON'T Quote SCHMUCKS!

edward michael o'durr supranowicz
Logan, USA

Cops

They are called that
probably because
They always cop a feel;
Always linger over
Your cock and balls,
Make sure there is
No weapon down there –
At least none
Larger than an official one.
They have the law
And give it to you
Like a corsage,
But such seduction
Is the only way
They get a date
Or suck your dick legally.

alan catlin
Schenectady, USA

Her t-shirt said,

BUMP and GRIND, gold lettering
on fading black and it looked
as if the shirt was made for a
much taller frame the way it
hung long at the arms and
shoulders, barely containing
the enormous bulk of her waist,
those thundering thighs only
a real Mack truck driving, hard
loving man could drive through,
an observation that leads me to
believe that the shirt's slogan
referred to his occupation as
an auto body repair man rather
than to hers as an exotic dancer.

jonathan brookes
Cardiff, Wales

Blessed

Arriving paperless that night
with little more to stand up in
and carry through to detention
than one gold tooth, I thought

myself at last among the blessed:
an Indian doctor tapped my chest,
a pretty lawyer from the Caribbean
in miniskirt and bangle earrings

brought documents for me to sign,
took them away again. And so, after
weeks of flying back and forth
across the world, I crossed

my fingers and began to plan
a future for myself along the lines
of the El Fayeds, till by the time
my deportation order was delivered

by dint of shrewd investment
and hard work, I'd built a chain
of castles in the air, each one
more splendid than the last. Now,

sandwiched in departures by a pair
of yawning policemen, I am aware
of flights ascending destination boards,
being called, then closed. Soon

these burly gentlemen will stand,
frogmarch me to the boarding gate
then, being English, shake my hand,
wish me a good flight, and wait

to see that I get on. Meanwhile
I watch with all the envy in the world
a black man push a polishing machine
back and forth across the floor.

s.harvey
Bolton, England

Gambling

They'll say you couldn't help yourself
so tried other means, as addicts do
to get what you wanted, me
i simply poured coffee as thick
as a thief, packed you off with a pony
left to lie like an idle wind-fall
upon the breakfast-table or stashed
in the empty underwear-drawer
then turned my back, emptily
kissed you across the threshold,
kept waving you on your way.

They'll try to make it up to me
as relatives do, try to cover your loss
pretending i didn't really know you
had it in you to stake everything
upon the world ending,
a fatal crash in stocks and shares,
a cup triumph for Hednesford.

It wasn't for nothing
i followed you to the edge
of town where the bookies swallowed
your pride but because the uncertain morning
our son first went to school alone when i shadowed
his reflection in a cold shop-window came back
to haunt me. I knew my job wasn't over
just because you thought you could
stand on your own two feet.

Heads, tails: i wasn't one
for gambling but i'd studied the form
from the credit agency, studied the form

from the court and bailiff too, knew the odds
were stacked against us, were longer
than any accumulator, the premium bonds
or those same six favourite numbers you clung to
each Saturday coming to our rescue. After all,
nothing was now worth the paper it was written on
except your life insurance and the betting slips
you suicidally poured your love and sorrow into
the moment before you rolled the die.

jon summers
Newport, Wales

Los Angeles or Southampton

Sit and watch
the night rise and fall.
Switch on the television.
Switch it off,
again.
Pour a can of lager.
Drink it,
and follow that up
with a glass of whisky
and then a couple more.
Put some music on.
Listen to it
for a while.
Stop.
Put the television back on
again
to make the room feel a little less empty.
Watch time pass.
Get ready for bed.
Piss.
Wash.
Sleep.

Wait for morning.
Wait for evening.
Wait for the weeks
to follow the days.
It's easy.

keith valentine
North Ferriby, England

Swarfega

I have a tin on a shelf in the garage
with orange cable wound around it
it's in there as still as treacle
fuming in an inch of air
under an industrial lid
only tools can remove
I keep it like my dad did
unopened
like a stash of adrenaline
cooling in a jar

on a Sunday afternoon
in 1976
when the blue paint on our box house
blistered in the sun
a Vauxhall Viva
slammed into the slope of the drive
like something falling from the sky
stopped by the earth
rocking on its hinges
with the clunk of hissing pipes

my dad slumped on the vinyl

his cheesecloth shirt
and every three inch square of denim on his jeans
covered in clotted ink

"get the swarfega boy"

he puked through the gap in the steering wheel
then slept

so I always keep a tin on a shelf
ready
just in case I need it
just in case my pen explodes

geoff stevens
West Bromwich, England

Epidemic

Telling them to go away has never been any good,
and stop-gap cures (like D.D.T.) lose their effectiveness.

The fact is, they like to run all over me,
stilling at times, so that I can see their features in detail,
from the markings and colourings, to the round shiny eyes,

but then, racing off again across my prickly skin,
leaving their tread in red weals, the reaction to their passage.

My nerve ends crawl with them;
they are super-bugs with the shock of cockroaches,
the germ-dirt, the frantic other-revved noise of buzzing flies.

They have bred to epidemic proportions.
I am earth. I am lousy with cars.

t. f. griffin
Leeds, England

Frank

Twenty years ago I remember his
Satin shirts, velvet jacket,
Clean-shaven good looks;
Now he's pointed to for his
Chest-length Old Testament beard,
Which he slowly twirls at its tip
While stopping mid-step, and standing
With the aspect of Archimedes
Pondering the spheres.

Twenty years on a permanently buttoned-up
Duffle-coat, hood up,
Keeps out the year's weather,
And a grimey green rucksack
Finishes the profile of a manifest integrity,
Undisturbed by the details of
Property or form. His hands work
Spade, shears, and the lifting
Of Special Brews, which oil the movements
Of his mind to its unshakeable centre.

As his gaze lifts from the ground
To speak, his eyes
(The whites of which are revolutionary red)
Lock into yours, and they expect nothing
Of you but truth.
What many fear I celebrate,
His stance of the Great Refusal,
An unimpeachable No,
Until he arrives on the other side.

brad evans
Cherry Hinton, England

**on
the last night
in
Spain**

my cock began
to itch

and I thought
of the

surfer I'd read
about in a

mag, who'd travelled
from

Australia and caught
some kind

of dick-rot

from
a Balinese hooker

and there was a
photo

showing a red stump
where

something else should've
been

and then I realised
that my

problem was a pair
of underpants

I'd been wearing 5 days
straight.

I solved the problem
by turning

them inside out,
it also eased

my
fear of

dick-rot.

graham hamilton
Hull, England

Beneath Black Ven Fossil Cliffs - 1999
(or one minute to midnight)

That thin line of rusted iron near the top
represents
when thinking began.

Those millions of layers of soft black shale
represent
things existing before thinking began.

Nice to have something so clear and
concrete

above a limitless sea of vast muddled
abstraction.

jonathan asser
London, England

Trick

All the guy did was steal
a stack of *News of the World*,
carting it off

by the blue twine binding.
Banged up with a lifer
who had an escape plan,

it just needed
the boy to agree
to have his arms tied

to the bunk.
You should have heard
the screams,

inmates pressing their bells,
asking the night screw
to please do something.

Professional Advice

The doctor told him
not to skip, and sure enough
he lost it all: the double

glazing, sofa too, some bathroom
fittings, handmade plants,
Venetian blinds, designer

toaster, shower curtain,
washing machine.
His world a stretch

of tarmac flanking the estate.
His rope a whirring blur
against the sky.

Progression

The images
have been in his mind
a long time,

but the head
in his freezer
is definitely real.

edward field
New York City, USA

Mirror Songs

1
When you look, fierce face, in the mirror mornings
is it absolutely necessary to groan?
It's not that you're ugly really, just old and ravaged
with, wouldn't you say, haunted eyes?
Well, you alone know what they've seen.

If your life has turned you into this, remember,
you've worked hard not to make it even worse.
Think of all the talking and screaming
therapies you've tried, not to mention acupuncture,
diet cures, years of yoga exercises,
and, as good as anything really, prayer.

Instead of hating your face, *shmeggege*,
can't you dredge up the least compassion
for what you've gone through? Tenderness, perhaps?
Don't scorn yourself. Give yourself a medal, pops –
it's been a long haul out of the pits, if you are out yet,
and you look it.

2
It takes nerve to live with hair like mine,
a Jewish frizz that defies the orthodoxy of goyish straight.
Some days, feeling shy, I groan
to see it, or what's left of it, in the mirror,
springing out around my gorgon head,
a giveaway, an impudence I'm not up to.

Tame it with scissors, comb, and oil,
inner voices say, and for years I obeyed.
Cut short and pasted down, it's a dimension less,
easier to live with and the world approves.
But is it me, the real me? Fuck you all,
don't I have the right to be beautiful?

In The Mirror

1
All day I look forward to that late hour
when I strip off clothes for exercises on a rug
woven, I am sure, by a jolly fat lady
who had the pattern in her mind but was divinely careless
as she chattered away with her friends at their looms.

This is my time to pay attention to important things:
In the wall mirror I gaze into my eyes
and as I move, study my body,
that map of a difficult childhood, a tortured ancestry –
it could be beautiful yet, I imagine,
and let it move as it wants to.

This is how, naked before a mirror,
I bend to the instructions in the carpet
in all possible directions, beyond the possible,
let breathing into every part of me again
until, inevitably, guided
toward caresses I didn't know I needed
I comfort myself with gentle hands.

2
On the field of an Oriental rug,
its symbols woven so as to move in the eye,
fragments of a forgotten writing, perhaps, an old knowledge,
their convolutions, by some mysterious process,
helping me move well,
teaching me balance....

Within the elaborate borders
are rows of figures called flowers in Persian,
not one exactly like the other,
as each tree dances differently in the wind
according to the nature of its leaves.

If the woven flowers are all lopsided,
there may be a perfect one in heaven, the rug says,
but that is unattainable here.
We don't have to be perfect either,
just make stabs at it.

Don't worry, the rug seems to say as I lift my arms,
if you collect all the flowers in your eye
they'll correct each other there into a perfect one
and do the work that they are meant to –
directing your body to move as if in the garden again,
and reminding you what you forgot –
that you're a dancer.

Over Fifty

It wasn't until I was over fifty
that I started to understand
life is divided into two parts,
and no more young, I saw
that I was in the half now that included
the retired, the feeble and wornout
inmates of nursing homes
and prostate, colostomy, and senility wards –
in short, THE WORLD OF THE OLD and all that means
rather than THE WORLD OF YOUTH the whole world celebrates.
It's enough to make one grumpy
if not be cause for trembling –
it's clear these are the last
days of my life.

Not that there aren't survivors –
let's not ask for looks, but with luck
some keep mind and spirit, though that's no consolation
when you walk through the sex bazaar of the streets
unwanted and ignored,
a zero.

Most people in my half of life are like
ships floundering in a gale
with hatches warped, valves stuck and everything leaking.
Now and then one sinks fast and is never seen again –
a lot are going down these days.
Already I can see that nothing is going to work right for long –
the warping, sticking, and leaking has begun
and it does no good to complain to doctors.
What can you expect, old boy, they say,
you're over fifty.

236

Of course, most of the body still works fine
but that's not what you die of.
It's from the one thing that doesn't,
even if all the rest is perfect.
But dying's another question, and just now
it's not HOW TO DIE,
but HOW TO LIVE UNTIL THEN
that drives me nightly, no matter how tired,
to my exercises, designed to ward off disaster one more day,
the motive – pure terror.

Nascent mathematician, I find myself subtracting my age
from the age in obituaries,
and I've suddenly become proprietor of a body
with a whole new set of problems.
Perhaps like in every other stage of life
they aren't solved, you just leave them behind,
except for the number one problem, How to Be Loved.

How far off now seem Being Popular
and What to Be When I Grow Up,
and grown up, What to Do with My Life, and above all,
How to Cope With the Insatiable Demands and Complications of Sex,
which always seemed the answer to meaninglessness,
the solution for feeling unwanted,
and the best excuse for not getting a job –

though the more I tried to make sex THE SOLUTION
the more miserably it failed,
until the time came, 0 my friends,
when desire that once needed to be restrained needed encouragement,
and in fact became recreational,
or anyway, rather than a sex-fiend obsession,
whatever it is now it's not crucial to going on.

Like quitting smoking, that leaves you
a lot more time on your hands,

though with time, as Berryman said, "rushing like a madman forward," there's nowhere to stop and think it all over.

This is an entirely different thing than life prepares you for, nor are there any instructions for what's ahead.

brendan cleary
Newcastle, England

The Reunion

MUUUHHH! she exclaims so theatrically
planting a big sloppy one on my cheek
after a year meeting outside Franco's.

That means 'don't even think about it',
still half-way through the ice-cream
I imagine a drop of it just slithering.

She fixes me with that pained expression;
'No Post-Mortems, Friends, we agreed'
so my fingers & eyes call for the bill.

The Neighbour

In some weird yoga position,
transcendental music playing,
she waves down from her window.

I'm stumbling, rubbing my eyes,
nipping around The Convenience
for biscuits, maybe streaky bacon.

How did she get to be so pure,
like she lives on a perfect cloud,
has the secret to levitate?

I imagine her spare apartment
on the way back with a 20-pack,
not a CD out of place, neat racks.

Later over Scottish John's coffee,
thick, a line of Speed stirred in,
I even consider her air-freshener.

I consider the gleam of her tiles,
a lack of stray hairs everywhere,
the ideal ambience to meditate.

Scottish John has rolled a stinker
& the cans piled up in the kitchen
will still be crying there tomorrow.

There's always stains on my underwear,
I'm sick of this, I'll march up there,
she'll be reading Tarot, a spotless bed.

I'll crash in somewhat worse for wear
& knock over her Japanese reading lamp:
'What makes me dirty?' I'll demand to know.

The Debate

'Just getting pissed all the time'
is Brian from Bray's theory
but I immediately take issue.

Explain yourself further, Brian,
M.A. Philosophy me, so discuss,
references, Brian, hard facts!

His eyes are whirling about:
'Let's crack a few cans first,
that's the core of my belief'.

The Economy

After his session with Marcus down the Hotspur
MR Woodford & myself are discussing banks & debt.

'Stout is the future, Sir!' he once bellowed
drowning out Sly Stone's Family Affair on the jukebox.

& once after 13 Gin Rickies Mr Woodford just vanished,
we found him asleep on the bog and hosed him down.

Mr Woodford & myself have 14 credit cards between us
but neither of us have any credit so we're moaning.

Then he tells me how Morris has just blagged a loan:
'Lombard, Sir, they gave Morris money for Tequila,

I mean the fuckin' banks can bale out Russia too
but not 2 decent lads like us just wanting scoops!'

'I couldn't agree more, Martin', I'm slurring again,
so we put our heads together, hatch another scam.

joseph allen
Ballymena, Northern Ireland

McFaul's Day

Bedsprings, bacon
McFaul at breakfast
looking over the milk-jug -
another empty day.

McFaul watches convent girls
kissing boys
green summerseats
white thighs, cigarettes.

After tea, McFaul tuts
the going-ons
in the public park.

The Foreman

He told me once
about sharing a bed
in digs in London,
how he kept moving away
as the boy pushed against him,
until, his back to the wall he obliged,
no other way out he laughed.

Called his wife the budgie,
described how she arched her back
doing the crab,
getting excited as the other men
watched her skirt ride up.

Once, while working in a quarry,
hand-picking stones for building,
scrambling back to safety from a landslide,
I rushed back,
pulling him clear,
as he was struck by rocks.

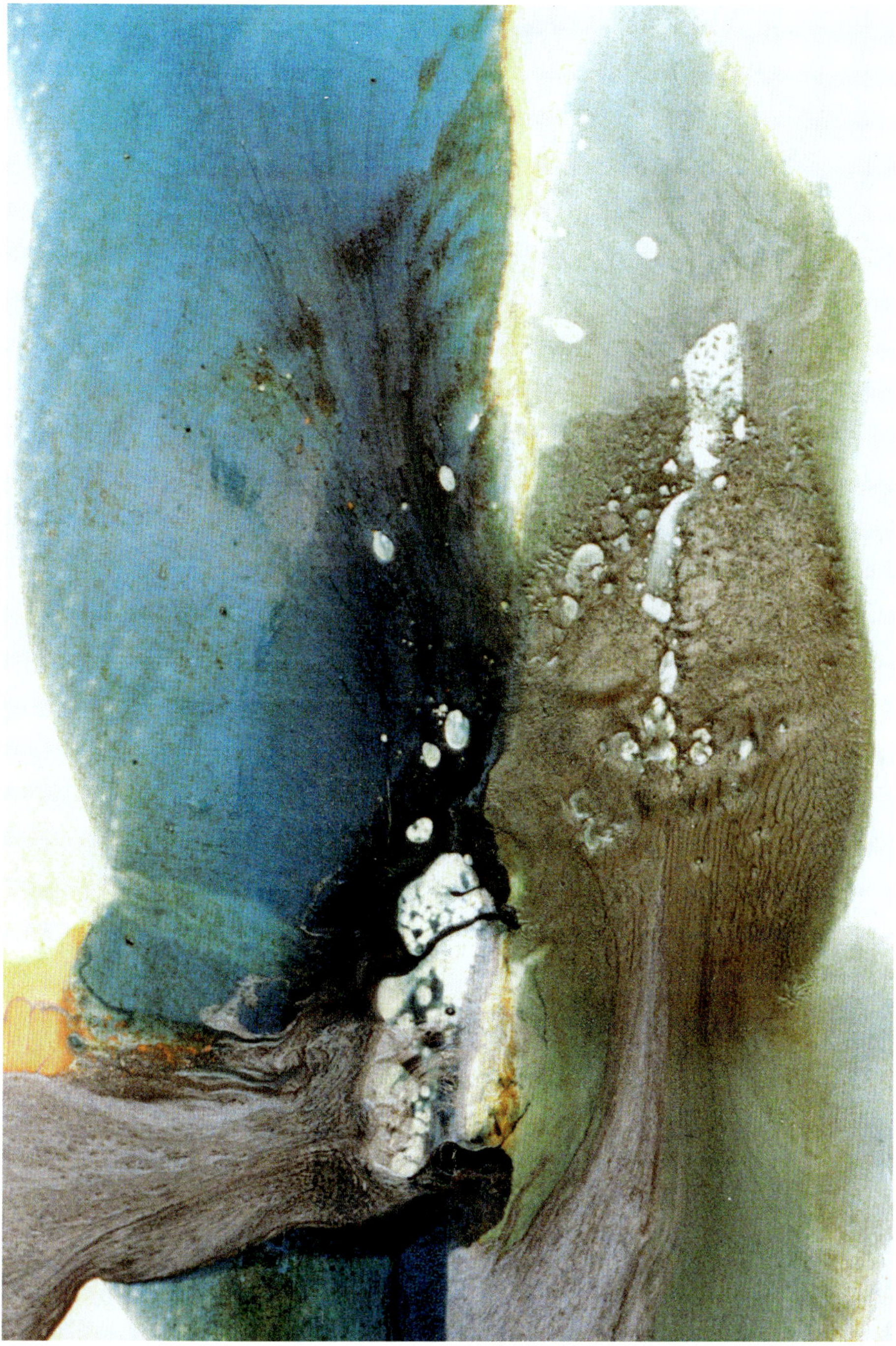

fiona curran
London, England

Jazz Lover

Is it Sonny, or was it Monk
that said, Jazz is in the genes,
I see that now we've met,
as surely as Miles came before
and between us. But you Coleman,
may I call you that ?
kissed me with a tenor sax tender,
hitting the pelvic dance floor
in all the right paces.
Swing day for night,
blow me in and out,
like the warm Missouri wind
which flew to your lips, unaided,
when first you made a play.
Make like love to me, for today
you have replaced all others,
every Art and Bud and Charlie,
they have gone the way
of easy, pillow lovers;
And so I am devoted, gentle Hawk
to only you. That breath,
slow, slow, now Coleman,
soft draw and fill me.

From The Front

There have been trip wires, booby traps
around you for so long, that now the ceasefire
may move towards permanent peace
and the walls come down, I do not know
what to do with you, comrade.
You who I've worked towards, so patiently,
searching for the delicate detente
I suspect rests somewhere in the gulf.
Negotiation has been almost impossible,
you stick to your well oiled guns,
all possible weapons remain at hand
when dealing with me, I who swear
to employ only reasonable force;
Yet you accuse me of charm like it was
the beginning of nuclear winter.
Is it only that you are afraid of peace,
that war suits you so much better,
calling all parties to your defence
assuming its necessity, then digging in,
for the duration of the siege,
while love is atrophied for lack of supplies.
This war is not civil, lover,
and I don't ask for surrender, I ask only
for permission to put in my ships
and lay off harbour. Concede this one thing,
my war time sweetheart, for my part,
I will if I must, be faithful, even
to your despot self.

don winter
Michigan, USA

Cleaning Up At The Hamtrack Burger Chef

Nights at this place
boss lines spray bottles up
across the counter. He says the red's
for shelves, the blue's for toilets,
and the white's only for
stainless steel. His eyebrows frown, but when
that bastard disappears into his office
I spray what I want
onto what I want.
Some nights his wife lifts
her ass onto the counter. She points
out turnover skins I missed.
Looks like she's been slept in
for years. Those nights I time
his trip to the bank to chase
her with the white bottle.
And I catch her and squeeze
the little Chef faces stitched
over her breasts. Some nights,

that is. But most nights the boss
looks right through me. His wife mechanically
cleans the salad bar, and yells
at the bits of mustard and dressing.
As if they are to blame
for all this. Most nights I turn up
the radio and sing my own words.
Something about being in this business to stay
alive. Something like that.

Saturday Night Desperate

We talked about it at the time clock
while we waited to punch in,
how it must have been the moon
looking half-starved and the radiator whiskey
brought us to her those Saturday nights,
and how the dog with the bowling ball
head barked from her front porch, back legs braced
to charge, front legs braced to turn
and retreat, and how a willow wept
its long springy tears over the tarpaper roof,
and how she came hard
out that door hung from one low
hinge and was on you, smelling
of possum, with slick hair and a cunt
with whiskers stiff enough to grate cheese,
and how she pitched her head back, buttoned
those green eyes and shook out punk
birdcalls under her shower cap, and how afterwards
we took turns with her in the outhouse,
the door swung half open, the lime-scented life
of the toilet seeping through
the half-moon cut in one wall, and we nodded
each other daft, winked and said *she's all that
and a bag of chips*, or something like that,
and what we left out was the only
thing true: how she laid back when she finished
with us, yawned like some cat
curled in the last pocket
of a threadbare afternoon, the dull book
of a dead moth loose in its paws.

michael gregg michaud
Los Angeles, USA

Tim's Wife Becomes A Lesbian And A Yoga Instructor

It took us a while to talk. Awkward.
I hadn't seen him in several months.
I sat on his vinyl couch and looked at an art book.
I need to read it, Tim said. I need to give it back.
He took a dulcimer from the closet and played it
cradled in his lap.
It's a mountain dulcimer, he said
without looking up.
We talked about art
and his ideas about decorating this new house
he rented in Echo Park.
It's a little sterile, he said.
And I need to fix those stairs. Paint a little.
Maybe some drapes, he added,
gazing at the sheet tacked over the window.
His wife had left him.
She became a lesbian and a yoga instructor.
She became a lesbian first.
He looked at the paper bag on the floor by my feet.
What are we waiting for? He asked. Drink no wine before it's time?
He opened the bottle, and we drank Merlot
while he showed me his studio filled with paintings
leaning against the walls. Pencil drawings on paper on a table.
I'm getting ready to do some new work, he said.
I just have a feeling it will be good. I'll start pretty soon.
We sat on the front porch and drank. He smoked a cigarette.
There's two skunks who pass by here, he said.
That's a fig tree there. I've some already.
The moon was shining full.
I want to stay with you, I said.
Oh, he said.
After a moment, he added, the bedroom's cold
and pretty messy.
We undressed slowly, not looking at each other.
The floor is cold, he apologized as he slipped in beside me.

His body was warm.
His mouth tasted like cigarettes and wine. Hesitant.
My hand trailed along his stomach
and settled between his legs.
He responded to my touch
and the act incited my vertebrae to shatter.
With our faces together
I could only think of Jill
and the day she cried in my car
telling me she wanted to leave him.
Later we laid quietly
breathing heavily
and when the wind blew
the house creaked loudly.
After a while he pulled the blanket aside
and rolled away from me.
He walked across the room,
opened a window, and leaned out to smoke.
He was skinny with a soft belly.
I don't want you to get the wrong idea, he said,
exhaling and looking at the moon.
I just wanted to try this.
I *do* like you, though, he added quickly,
looking over at me watching him,
sitting up on my elbows in his bed.

In Defence Of Voyeurism

The radiator knocked
and I couldn't sleep because I knew
his window would be open.
From the top step into my rectangle of view
wearing boxers and athletic socks.
only when he sat at the desk facing
the window did I see his face,
too young for his chiseled body,
through the open venetian blinds.
He played with his curls while
he read a book, bit his pencil, drummed
it on the tabletop, and tried to write.
How many nights I've watched him,
dizzying stories in my head.
His twin bed visible and thin blanket
carefully smoothed he would lay
gleaming in the television light,
his perfect feet and ankles crossed,
arms folded behind his head.
I wondered what he was thinking, alone,
with stories of his own.
The warmth and scent of his room.
of the inviting shadow in the hollow
of his collarbone, his intricately
ridged abdomen, the movement of his foot
to some sound, some music. A song, if I
strained, I might have heard.
And then there was something shocking
about his nakedness when he stripped
for bed. His narrow hips, his full
white backside brushed by the tiny circle
of table light. Would I touch his hair,
turn his shoulders?
Desire can make anything real,
and longing delivers the object
of our desire not into our hands
but under our skin.

peter knaggs
Hull, England

In Praise Of Tin Openers

Like legs of scissors
or handles of clippers,
a butterfly key,
now a hard block of plastic,
a cog and a circular blade
to hook on the lip,
to puncture and pierce the rim,
to roll around clockwise,
a scooting incision
at the twist and wheel
of thumb and first finger.

Your only trustworthy utensil
west side of the kitchen
drawer, I'm telling you boy
for bareknuckled wing-nut
spinning he's your man,
the only apparatus
for unlocking
your aluminium exit,
not roughshod or jerky,
jagged or bodged,
no dastardly tricks,
flicking back like a pike,
splattering beans,
or nicking your finger.

No jack of all trades
this man's a specialist,
a tin cutting champion,
a kitchen drawer yardstick,
shove your melon-baller,
apple-corer, fondue kit,
your pizza cutting poncey
wedding gift gadgets.

Stick your kitchen drawer
clutterers, your waste of spacers,
no teflon midnight runner
or a fad that changes overnight
or breaks in the night,
not the latest newfangled
gizmo, got to have gimmick
from Lakeland Plastics,
give me a man I can trust
to open my soup
and call him Elvis.

The Door Bell Is Ringing

don't think of his brains
dashed out by half bricks,
four finger-shaped bruises
fruiting on the upper arm,
a wagless tongue, lolled
like a drunk horse,
a blue face, or a boot lace
drawn around the neck,
don't think about
his favourite superman
T shirt, disturbed,
or his tiny fractured finger
poking out like a twig,
from a shallow covering,
or the police Alsatian
sniffing in the brambles,
barking at the nettles,
and four policemen running
over, as slow as they can.

A Man On Chanterlands Avenue Slices An Onion

A size enough to hold in the hand,
to sit there nice, the fingers to shape
round it, like a bowler measuring
a yorker, he holds the weight of it,

of hearing it on the radio, Keegan
the little boy left in the pushchair
outside Jacksons, onion skin stretched
old suitcase tan, bright as linoleum,

Keegan missing, his mother hysterical.
He heard about it first on the radio
at work, and a row of tiny black
falling stars are pricking the root.

Equidistant thin wood lines under-wire
the papery wrapping, imagine it
your boy, measured as hand-made sweets,
smooth as chestnut, hard as turnip.

He pulls a knife across the onion top,
tipped by a scrunch of old document,
dry as dead flowers. On the front page
of the Hull Daily Mail was a photo

of the missing toddler and a headline,
before the onion is sliced its gentle
assault on the nose no more
than cricket match teas, a jar lid,

your fingers the day after cooking
"HULL BOY KEEGAN AGE 3 GOES MISSING
WHILE MOTHER GOES SHOPPING."
the onion skin, fissured, split,

reveals its sallow under-layer
bursting out of its shirt.

Sam Thumbs a Spent Cartridge Twenty Years After.

There used to be an advert
with the line, "A man's got to do
what a man's got to do."
That's why Sam is out on't moor
with a shovel and a gun,
a single sufficient cartridge,
a court order and his dog.
In his canvas bag
1/2 lb of best rump steak
and a hip flask for after.
Next dog he oughta call Cantona.
None of this, "It's alright love,
he dun't bite," more like,
"You better steer clear pet
he'll have your ruddy hand off."
Train him up a vicious bugger,
to snarl at folk, warn em off.
After spading out, right size hole,
changes his mind,
takes a sup of brandy,
                    beforehand.

dean wilson
Hull, England

The King And I

Is your flat
still a shrine to Elvis
or have you found
someone else to worship?

There was a time
when it looked like
I was in the running
until I fell at the first hurdle
after taking too much for granted

even so it was good while it lasted
and I'd happily go through
every second again
just for the hell of it

and do you still drive
that yellow van
with ladders on top
the one I climbed into
at the drop of a hat?

There's not a day goes by
when I don't think of that moment
and the afternoon at your place
going at it like there was no tomorrow

and does the old woman opposite
still cook your tea
and bring it across at five o'clock every single day
in exchange for doing the garden
and slaying any dragons that happen her way?

Shopping 1

The humming
of the escalator
is a voice that won't take
no for an answer

so a five fingered discount
is just what the doctor ordered
adrenalin served with relish
and a gap in the market cornered

Shopping 2

I'm in the mood for taking
leave of my senses
so get your glad rags on
I've got a pocket full of twenties

and while you're about it
let down your defences
now's as good a time as any
for living off the interest of our excesses

Shopping 3

I've got plenty
I'm so full I'm empty
so please don't tempt me
for I am twenty

thousand pounds in debt
on account of a spending spree
that isn't over yet

giovanni malito
Cork, Ireland

Cityscape #12

When the fog thinned
I wiped a peephole
into my window.
I looked down on a man
across the street.
He was standing
under the sign
of the Sports bar.
Suddenly,
his breast was stained
the dull red of a robin
and he crumpled.
His throat was cut.
Within seconds
a crowd gathered.
The ambulance came
and then it went.
Someone from the bar
appeared with a brush
and a bucket of water.
The blood was sluiced
down the drain
and the crowd went away.

Don't Cry for Me, Suburbia

The things that spill
out into the street –
howls and shrieks,
but sometimes, laughter,
Life at close quarters
on either side of paper walls
nothing can bring down.
And nothing can shock
anymore.
Our souls are insulated,
rated for at least
one million BTU's,
and our hearts are wire-
reinforced,
encased in pre-mixed
poured concrete.
They have shrunk
and have become
smaller than our fists.
Still, everyone weeps
for the baby born
3,000 miles away
without legs,
the stray dog run down
in the street, or a Princess
who gagged
on her silver spoon.
But who cries for you,
unwitting victim
of the absurd
hypocrisy of state...
I was going to rant
about various things,
but what's the point?
I'd gain nothing

but heartburn when
as pathetic as it sounds,
what I want to find
is a heart that burns.

Atlas Should Shrug

With age they come
and they come,
one after another.
First, there was no
Santa Claus, then
the tooth fairy proved
to have limited resources.
Miss Rowley,
my fifth grade teacher,
was engaged to be married
and she wasn't
really a blonde.
My father had never been
a cowboy, in fact
had never even been
on the back of a horse.
Father Vernelli
walked the downtown streets
checking out prostitutes.
Jim Morrison
treated Pamela like shit
and ABBA was a supergroup.
Freud was insecure
and a University degree
guarantees nothing.
And still, they come
and they come
one after another
but frankly,
I no longer give a shit.

susan maurer
New York City, USA

Lemurs

She ate him with her eyes
With the teeth of her eyes
She ate his face
Dragging the rake of her eyes, the tiller
Down his face
How was he this morning
Trust for him
Was a broken spoon
Although your hands were loving
You do not love me
This morning, you wish me gone
I need travel directions
They say
"Please hold on, the line is busy
This is not a disconnect. A silent period will follow
And then a transit person will answer."
I said goodbye
But you had left
Into your pleasant self
Your eyes were turned off
Last night I dreamt of lemurs
And today the images
Sweep my mind in dragnets
Hooking here and there
I said goodbye
But you were on another channel
And so I left in the rain
A stock situation
I with a blinded lemur in a box
As directional device
Last night I dreamt of lemurs
Navigation is tricky
I think as I leap puddles to get to the curb

Starstreak

I took some stars from my pocket
And gave them to you
Certain it was the one thing you'd want the most
0 they were not accurate
Stars are not gold, with five points
And stick-on like teacher gives
Stars are more white really, no dust at all, I believe

I thought stars might anneal your sense
Of being a sexual mayfly, mouthless
Thought it might lift the sense you have
Of being an obligate swimmer
Shark that must swim or die
This knowledge in the cartilage
Blind and driven
You licked one, stuck it on your cheek
A beauty mark, went on with the party
All my ministrations were bootless
You were swept away

Mackie Hill, Miami, Arizona

When I was a kid
Dogs ran free
There were dogfights
Chow-chow and
Bonzo
On Mackie Hill
I used to fall a lot
My knees were always skinned
Little girls wore skirts
Whistling women and crowing hens
Come to bad ends
Gramma said, 0
Anima, animus
I dreamt of her last night
And brushed my hair 100 times
(I'd visit her if she were here)
She told me to each night
There was terror
Lest we forget
The boys tied a donkey
In the path of the lava/slag
They dumped each night
From the copper mine
Which killed Bill

THE QUEST and SELECTED POEMS
(pamphlet and CD) Tony Griffin
(The Attic Rooms)
reviewed by Ian Parks

It starts with the publication of *A Rumoured City* by Bloodaxe in 1982. Edited by Douglas Dunn and with a foreword by Philip Larkin, the anthology launched the careers of, among others, Peter Didsbury, Tony Flynn, Sean O'Brien, Dougas Houston, and set the agenda for their work during the next decade. From the beginning, and from the selection that appeared in *A Rumoured City*, it was obvious to predict that Tony Griffin was going to prove to be something of a literary maverick - and this has certainly proved to be the case. While closely associated with the Hull poets, Griffin has always stood slightly on the outside of that grouping, sharing the occasional affinity but stubbornly working out a path of his own. Dunn's valuable estimation of Griffin's work as 'mystical and visionary' drew immediate attention to one very important aspect of his approach but failed to highlight what seem to me to be his greatest virtues as a poet: his unflinching eye for detail and his inherent integrity, both of which are demonstrated to good effect in *The Quest* and on *Selected Poems*.

Compared with his contemporaries, Griffin has been slow to develop his characteristic style. Not until the publication of his first full collection. *Cider Days*, by Headland in 1990 did Griffin achieve anything approaching his full potential or distinctive voice. Reviewing it for *Bete Noire* (in the Hull Poets special edition in 1992) Peter Didsbury was keen to isolate 'the whole of Griffin's concern' which he identified as an attempt 'to chart the struggle towards the acts of faith by which, faced with annihilation, one chooses, and *decides to continue to choose*, love. I wouldn't want to qualify that statement; but perhaps suggest that Griffin arrives at this point by working *through* a series of precise and concrete images in order to recreate certain emotional states. And with *The Quest* Griffin appears to have consolidated his true voice: assured, idiosyncratic, particularised, moving – and, at times, capable of deep insights into what it means to be human. 'Love is an absence' Griffin states in the opening line of *The Loss*. Elsewhere, as in *Adel Crag*, he seems to be moving into the sort of territory once occupied by the late Jon Silkin:

'The days lent their appearances to us
As we moved towards change -
This was a love song,
Unmoved by distance,

Challenged, broken, and new.

And indeed *Adel Crag* proves to be one of the highlights of *Selected Poems* in which Griffin reads in a measured, deliberate style, constantly open to the variations and nuances implicit in his verse. He brings a disarming sensitivity to bear on personal poems such as *The Photograph* which opens the selection, and a degree of invective to the more 'public' pieces like *Cider Days*. A few well-chosen words of introduction precede some poems but never confuse the listener with a welter of background material. So many poets disappoint when they give readings of their own work, Griffin's assured, careful performance actually serves to elucidate the poems themselves, adding a further dimension and clarity to the audience's appreciation. His recent reading at the 1999 Hull Literature Festival with Peter Didsbury and Andrew Motion afforded ample evidence of his confidence as both a poet and a reader of his own work.

Sometimes Griffin has a tendency to reach for and feel entirely at ease with the obvious image – usually stars; sometimes his sense of rhythm lapses momentarily. And yet, for a poet who balances so precariously between metre and free-verse these apparent weaknesses often add to the overall impression of immediacy. Griffin is, in many ways, a pure poet who remains unaffected and unconcerned by current trends and fashions in contemporary poetry. His continued imperviousness and tenacity make for a true poet who is constantly alert to his own potential, who develops from one poem to the next, and whose best work is probably still to come.

REPAIR, C. K. Williams (Bloodaxe) £7.95
reviewed by Graham Hamilton

C.K. Williams' poems have an easy going confident immediacy, such that the insights which he leads you on to seem as if they have been happened upon; commonplace yet revelatory, surprising and yet familiar.

His core themes are the all too human aspects of what it is to be human, often dealt with in a uniquely painstaking fashion. Many of these delicate explorations go deep into the interstices of humankind's experience in exacting detail . The writing deepens our own experience by an implicit challenge to confront our inner life as has done; a challenge to sound the depths of our own insights, to look more clearly, more honestly, and by doing so, to take the care to live more fully. He is exploring the boundary conditions of human possibility and saying that this is what life can be.

In a formal sense what he offers us here is an unfaltering display of his mastery of a wide range of differing styles of verse encompassing different subjects, objects and persons. The short lyric, the discursive narration, philosophical and psychological meditations are all carried of with enviable aplomb.

What distinguishes and elevates his writing above the technical is his ability to capture the reader with moments of surprised recognition; a sheer correctness of delineation which delivers a bristling shock of exultation. Time and again he delivers the kind of instants that remind you forcibly of the times that poetry first did that for you. It is this which makes him a prime contemporary candidate for the appellation "great" rather than the just "very good" or "excellent".

Much of his of poetic greatness is really a romantic greatness, of the tradition set out in *Lyrical Ballads*, which might be caricatured as the elevation to the poetic level of mundane subject matter. In the twentieth century Larkin was a prime exemplar of this technique in what might be termed his "High Windows" mode; a relatively plain yet careful description of ordinary things happening is at some point given a surprisingly epiphanous twist.

Williams does similar things in his own way; a poem such as *Droplets* for example fuses familiar images of rain on leaves on the balcony and piano music in the room beyond into an image which is simultaneously a moment of acceptance of mortality and of such mortal moments as being all that we have, as well as regret for the fact that they in time will be lost. Again; in *Ice*, the first piece in the book, a finely drawn description of the shattering of an ice block leads to the fantasy that the shattering might be reversed

> ... *the mass reconstituted, with precious little of*
> *its brilliance lost,*
> *just this lucent shimmer on the rough, raised grain of water-rotten floor,*
> *just this single drop, as sweet and warm as blood, evaporating on your tongue.*

There is much of this well wrought, thoughtful, singing language throughout the book. There are however other modes in which Williams is equally enthralling. In poems such as *The Dress*, *The Poet*, and most stunningly in, *King*, his style is open, conversational. You feel almost like you're in the kitchen sharing anecdotes and beer. For example, *The Poet* begins:-

> *I always knew him as 'Bobby the Poet', though whether he ever was one*
> *or not,*
> *someone who lives in words, making a world from their music, might be a*
> *question.*

This directness is, of course, harder to achieve than it looks, especially as when in this poem things get a little more intense. Williams turns it around and conveys powerfully the inherent insecurity and mental anguish at the heart of many attempts at artistic endeavour.

Even more anguish is apparent in *King* , an indelible memoir from 1968 of the day of the memorial service for the murdered civil rights leader Martin Luther King. In this piece the social, racial and political tension of the events are exemplified in a personal drama which resonates powerfully and with profound sadness thirty years later.

The narrator of the poem has arranged to attend the service with a black friend who is, in sight of the narrator, the victim of aggressive racial harassment by white police men. The black man turns his justifiable rage against his white friend:-

Don't tell me you know what I feel, and don't give me that crap about being
    with us
you wouldn't know how to be with us, you don't know the first thing about us
 For three hundred years we've coddled you, protected your illusions of innocence,
Letting you go on thinking you're pure, well you're not pure you're the same as
    those pigs.
And please, please don't tell me again you can understand because you're a Jew.

The plain shock of these lines stays with you as the memory of them has stayed with the writer:

I can still feel your anger, feel still because it's still in me my helpless
    despair.

In *After Auschwitz* and *The Nail* Williams again turns to the problem of how the individual can respond to events of extraordinary prejudice and horror. How to go on as human being in the face of what we humans are capable of? No poetry after Auschwitz? He sees that place of horror as:-

> *Not risen from its ruins*
> *but caught in them forever*
> *it demands of us how*
> *we'll situate this so*
> *it doesn't sunder us*
> *between forgivenesses*
>
> *we have no right to grant*

In *The Nail* he tells of a dictatorship in which

the way his henchmen had disposed of enemies was by hammering
nails into their skulls

and recognises that

Its we who do such things, we who set the slant, embed the tip, lift the

> *sledge and drive the nail*

This willingness to look at the totality of what is human is a great strength, and the balance required is achieved in other poems such as *The Dance* in which the tenderness and beauty of existence are allowed lines such as

> *that world beyond us which so often disappoints, but which sometimes shows*
> *shows us, lovely, what we are.*

This is both daring in its unabashed lyricism and uplifting in a way which is not crassly sentimental. Williams' poetry is ultimately one of hope, of optimism.

Another strand is the atavism so prevalent in the post – industrial consciousness. No better exemplified by poems of deliciously articulated anthropomorphism such as *Shock* in which an animated and vicious scrapyard crane is compared to

> *... a crow*
> *with less evident emotion*
> *punches its beak through the dead*
> *breast of a dove or albino*
> *sparrow...*

Here, the writer seems to be saying that perception is all, that we create the world as we wish to see it. Such reflections on cognition, consciousness, the self, and, even, that supposed remnant of a redundant metaphysic, the soul, are evident in several poems. In *Not Soul* for example the soul

> *is what even the most skeptical still save for any resolving description*
> *of inner life, this intricately knotted compound*
> *which resists any less ambiguous locution.*

Such reflections on the nature of mind provide some of the most impressive writing in the book. The sheer acuity of his phenomenological observations and the precise economy with which he communicates on matters which by their very nature are complex and fleeting is enthralling.

*A self which by definition cannot tell
itself untruths, yet lies, which, wanting
to leal itself untruths, isn't able to, not then,
and would like sometimes not to know
it's lied, but can't deny it has, not then.*
                                         from The Lie.

This is a book in which it 'is difficult to find a line which seems misplaced; all the poems are realised superbly in their differing ways and at the centre of all of them is a superb and unique poetic voice.

cd contents:

1	brendan cleary -	the economy
2		peter
3		the resident
4		the debate
5		the neighbour
6		the reunion
7		the lodger
8	ian parks -	tiger lillies
9		navigation road
10		unicorns
11	devreaux baker -	ghost trains
12		song of belfast
13		nights in the north sea
14		homesick
15		myself greets you
16	dean wilson -	adidas
17		graham
18		my sheffield prince
19	daithidh maceochaidh -	the kipper's shanty - (plus car alarm j)
20	graham hamilton -	beneath black ven fossil cliffs
21	lisa glatt -	what the fast girl says
22		in this foul alley
23		i will see their teeth
24		hungry
25	peter knaggs -	the radio
26		suckers
27	joan jobe smith -	ah, memories, memories
28		L.A. luv
29	seamus curran -	drac
30		taxi ride
31		good friday
32		language lessons
33	fred voss -	with machine grease on my pants
34		my fan
35		dickwads
36	carol coiffait -	brave
37		hide and seek
38	labi siffre -	six of the best
39		chips
40	gerald locklin -	beer